"DON'T GO, BUNNY." ALEC SAID, HIS HEART surging with yearning. "Stay."

"Stay and do what?" She felt that stirring again, a feeling of fighting to escape from a dungeon. It was scary enough to send a shiver through her body.

Alec enfolded her in his arms, whispering, "Stay and make love to me princess." He laughed softly. "You want me, too, don't try to say you don't. Stay, and we'll make love all night long."

Curling her arms around his neck, Bunny looked into his face, made more handsome by the shadows. Her body ached with need, pressed against his. She searched Alec's face, her doubts stonger than her desires. "I don't think one night with a man like you would ever be enough."

He ached to offer her the world, the universe, but did he dare risk his heart? He whispered, "I've got lots of nights. . . ."

WHAT ARE *LOVESWEPT* ROMANCES?

They are stories of true romance and touching emotion. We believe those two very important ingredients are constants in our highly sensual and very believable stories in the LOVESWEPT line. Our goal is to give you, the reader, stories of consistently high quality that may sometimes make you laugh, sometimes make you cry, but are always fresh and creative and contain many delightful surprises within their pages.

Most romance fans read an enormous number of books. Those they truly love, they keep. Others may be traded with friends and soon forgotten. We hope that each LOVESWEPT romance will be a treasure—a "keeper." We will always try to publish

LOVE STORIES YOU'LL NEVER FORGET
BY AUTHORS YOU'LL ALWAYS REMEMBER

The Editors

Loveswept ® 657

FEVER

JOAN DOMNING

BANTAM BOOKS
NEW YORK · TORONTO · LONDON · SYDNEY · AUCKLAND

FEVER

A Bantam Book / December 1993

*If you would be interested in receiving protective vinyl covers for your
Loveswept books, please write to this address for information:*

> Loveswept
> Bantam Books
> P.O. Box 985
> Hicksville, NY 11802

> ISBN 0-553-44281-3

Published simultaneously in the United States and Canada

Bantam Books are published by Bantam Books, a division of Bantam Doubleday Dell Publishing Group, Inc. Its trademark, consisting of the words
"Bantam Books" and the portrayal of a rooster, is Registered in U.S. Patent
and Trademark Office and in other countries. Marca Registrada. Bantam
Books, 1540 Broadway, New York, New York 10036.

PRINTED IN THE UNITED STATES OF AMERICA

OPM   0 9 8 7 6 5 4 3 2 1

For Beth,
the beautiful and beloved Bitsybuss.
My last, but far from least.

ONE

Alec Golightly had to laugh when he received another desperate summons to come to the front office. Not that there was anything funny about an efficiency expert arriving to evaluate the company for the new owner. It was no wonder the boss needed moral support. He left the packaging department in the questionable hands of his special troop and walked across the kit-furniture-factory grounds under an overcast sky.

In the main building, balding Henry Fosse was pacing a path in the threadbare rug in his office. "I'm too old to cope with the Woodbox getting caught in a furniture manufacturer's buyout," he burst out when Alec walked in. "If you'd taken over as general manager when the board asked you to, I could've retired and been off fishing now."

"Management isn't me," Alec said, twitching his swashbuckling brown mustache.

"Baloney, you're giving up too damn much for those people in Packaging. The least you could have done is put on a jacket."

The twitch turning into a grin, he tucked his green-and-blue-flowered Hawaiian shirt in his jeans and propped a hip on the windowsill, stretching one long leg out. "I doubt a big-time efficiency expert will notice my fashion statement."

Henry whisked past in his pacing. "I know she's going to advise Eleganté Furniture to close us down. You've got a fancier tongue than me, maybe you can talk her around."

Alec shared Henry's anxieties. His smile faded. "Okay, I'll launch a campaign to save the Woodbox."

The other department heads arrived then, the men in jackets and a very pregnant Nan Turner in a dress. Henry turned his worries toward them, and Alec turned his toward the window, gazing at a log ship moving down the Columbia River toward the ocean. If he had his boat finished, he could have sailed off into the wild blue yonder, which sure would have beat wondering what his special troop would do if the Woodbox went under.

A red sports car rolled into the parking lot and stopped near the window. He came abruptly to attention when a woman emerged to walk in a symphony of motion to the door. Her body was aerobically lithe: hips slender, breasts perky, and waist tiny under a wide belt. Even at a distance, he could see her face was stunning behind gold-framed glasses, her hair a mane of melted amber.

She looked like a movie star, but they weren't expecting one of those.

Moments later the intercom blared, "Miz Bernice Fletcher is here." Seconds after that she came striding into the office, flashing a one-hundred-watt smile. "Spare me the Bernice, please, I answer to Bunny."

Alec had never seen anyone who looked less like a Bunny. Her briefcase spoke of power; her peacock-blue jumpsuit and gold jewelry were stylish and sophisticated and smacked of designer expensive. He doubted even he could talk this woman around.

Smooth and cool as ice cream, she shook hands and repeated names as Henry introduced himself, the others, and finally, "Last but not least, the fellow on the windowsill is Alec Golightly, head of Packaging."

Her eyes were large and delft blue with thick lashes behind the chic glasses. They narrowed judgmentally at his colorful shirt and widened ever so slightly at his lusty mustache. Then she chilled him with an impersonal PR smile. "Mr. Golightly. What an unusual name."

He came forward with a friendly grin, hoping to mellow her toward the Woodbox, maybe toward himself, too, with his usual teasing informality. "I expect I had English forebears who went lightly in and out of some questionable activities."

She didn't give his little joke so much as a wry smile. No sense of humor? An ice maiden? Bad news. Luckily she was smaller than her attitude, the top of her head level with his chin. Being tall gave him an edge, but only until he shook hands. Then a sort of magic flowed from her soft hand to his callused one, turning him to jelly. All he could do was stare down at her, a goofy grin frozen on his lips.

To his delight, she wasn't immune either. Pink spots the size of silver dollars popped out on her cheekbones. Jerking her hand free, she began to take off her glasses, then shoved them back on. Though he couldn't imagine why he'd set her off. He wasn't anywhere near her league, his face bland, if not downright ugly, nose flattened and chin scarred. Unfortunately she pulled her icy control around herself and turned to Nan Tur- ner. "You're in charge of the business office, perhaps you'd show me to a computer. I'd like to get started on my job."

Inner reactions aside, Alec couldn't allow her to think of the Woodbox as a trifling job, and launched his campaign. "Miz Fletcher, we'd like to know if your credentials qualify you to decide the fate of our fifty-some employees."

"I won't be making decisions, only writing a report," she said quickly, then looked at each worried face as if realizing for the first time that she might affect someone's fate. "But if it makes you feel more secure, I have a degree in computer science, an MBA, and ten years' experience running a business in Los Angeles. Wilderness Enterprises."

Alec's brows shot up. "You mean Wilderness Enterprises as in nature films and a major movie about Native Americans?" At her nod, he gave a low whistle, realizing she was a business dynamo. "If you ran a multimillion-dollar business, what in hell are you doing in a place like this?"

Her features tightened in a spasm of pain. "I'm with a consulting firm now, under contract to evaluate the— uh—" Her face went blank.

"The Woodbox," he supplied, light bulbs going off in his mind. Consulting meant she was a dynamo at loose ends. Exactly what the Woodbox needed in its time of crisis. Besides that, the notion of seeing this beautiful woman every day, maybe thawing her frozen shell, was fascinating. He sighed over the impossible dream. "I'm not surprised a woman of your experience might have trouble remembering the name of a little subsidiary factory like ours. Right—uh—Bunny?"

She gave him an irritated glance. "Don't let my name, my experience, or my appearance fool you, Mr. Golightly. Eleganté sent the best, and I'll do your factory justice. Consider yourself fortunate."

"Yes, Miz Fletcher, I do consider myself blessed," Alec avowed, an appeasing smile tilting his mustache. "I've always been partial to brilliant, successful women."

For some reason his effort at appeasement made her even angrier. Her eyes and voice dripped icicles. "Fortunately my job doesn't depend upon what you are or aren't partial to."

Oblivious to undercurrents, Henry threw another bug into the floundering campaign by laughing. "Our Alec is partial to a lot of interesting things, but he's not the lightweight that shirt might lead you to believe. He's been with the Woodbox since he was sixteen. Eleven years. Spent time in each department during high school, came back permanent after college. So he's the perfect choice to take you on a grand tour of the factory."

Bunny shook her head, agitating spiraled curls. "No! A tour isn't time-efficient. Eleganté gave me two days max, and it'll take that long to research your records."

Alec stepped forward and heated up the pressure. "The records won't tell you how efficiently the operation is run or what kind of employees work here." He lifted his brows. "You *are* interested in the people?"

She had no choice but to say, "Of course I am."

Walking to the open door with everyone's gaze on him, he looked back, a smug grin twitching his mustache. "Then let's not waste any more of your limited time."

Bunny's lips curved in a smile of admiration for his tactics. Her musky perfume wrapped around him as she brushed through the door. "You win," she murmured for his ears only. "This time." Outside the office, she ducked into a rest room.

Alec leaned on the wall, plotting his campaign. The ultimate goal was talking Bunny Fletcher into lending her expertise on an extended basis, or at least into writing a glowing report. As for his more ignoble goals, he decided treating this particular woman to his harmless habit of flirting could be a deadly mistake. Taboo.

When Bunny came out again, he'd steeled himself against seeing her hair fluffed into a golden halo around a flawless face, and her body svelte under the jewel-blue jumpsuit. But it threw all his noble resolutions out of whack to see the ice maiden blow a gum bubble. "A few minutes in the john did wonders for your attitude," he murmured.

She lifted an aristocratic chin. "I've never been in a *john* in my life."

"Right."

Cursing himself for his lapse, Alec escorted her outside. Streams of sunlight were piercing the clouds. The air was scented by the river, sawdust, and pine forests. The four barrackslike factory buildings were painted a clean pale yellow, landscaped with evergreens and bushes.

Planting a hard hat on his head at the entrance to the warehouse, he handed Bunny another and started the tour. To his surprise, as they made their way through Manufacturing and Maintenance, she showed a genuine interest in pressed board, power saws, and laminating, asking dozens of technical questions about the production of do-it-yourself kit furniture.

Last on the agenda was his own domain. Alec scuffed his work boots on the path. "I'd better explain something before we go into Packaging and Delivery. I have about twenty people working for me, but a baker's dozen of them have mild to moderate developmental handicaps."

She stopped chewing her gum to assimilate the information. "You mean they're retarded?"

"Yes." Defensive as a new father when it came to

his troop, he squared off in front of her. "I hope you can understand what a major contribution the Woodbox makes by giving them an opportunity to hold down jobs. They run into prejudice as soon as they're old enough to go out in public. There aren't many places where they can feel productive."

"Yes, I see that might be true." Bunny studied the passion blazing in his face. "Is there some reason you're so evangelistic on the subject?"

"Everyone has their causes," Alec said, not about to bare his soul and his secrets to a superior beauty. "Come inside and see how the furniture pieces are put together into kits."

Inside Packaging, Bunny peered into the huge room where the kits were being assembled. Several of the employees were counting screws, pulls, and handles into bags. Others were encasing bags, wood pieces, and instructions in plastic with shrink-wrap machines. Last, the product was cartoned under the Woodbox logo with a banging of staple guns.

Alec watched her anxiously, suspecting the success of his campaign was hanging on her reaction. "My special people range in age from eighteen to forty-three. Ten have Down's syndrome, two were brain-damaged at birth, and one picked up his flaw from the family genes."

"How sad and unfair," she said, her icy facade softening for the first time.

"You betcha." Taking her hand, he stepped into the

room. Thirteen pairs of hands paused in midmove and twenty-six artlessly adult eyes looked up. "I've brought a lady named Bunny to visit. Let's show her what a great job you do." Lowering his voice, he asked, "Do you feel up to meeting them personally?"

Bunny gazed out over the room for a moment, then glanced at him. "Are you wearing that awful shirt for them?"

Smiling wryly, he brushed at the riotous Hawaiian flowers on his chest. "They respond better when I look relaxed."

"I see." Discarding her hard hat, she dug in her brief-case for a clip and pulled her hair back. That, along with a bit of magic he didn't catch, turned the chilly beauty into a gentle woman with warm eyes and an engaging smile. "I'm ready to meet them now."

Astonished by the transformation, he led her to the first table. Jake, frightened of anything new, promptly spilled his pail of screws on the floor. She sat down and helped him pick them up, charming a smile out of him.

Alec's amazement and respect grew as she made the rounds of the room, seemingly unruffled by bizarre nervous habits. She didn't even flinch when Tess ran stubby, curved fingers over her jewelry, crooning, "Pretty lady."

"I'll tell you a secret," Bunny said, leaning forward with a smile. "I'm not really pretty, it's all pizzazz."

"Secret from the Golightly Man," Tess said with her slurring speech defect. "He looking gaga at you."

With her shields down, Bunny glanced at Alec's grin with a much warmer attitude. "The Golightly Man better mind his own business."

"We his business. He fixes our problems," Tess said. Then she glanced at a stocky man by a shrink-wrap machine. "I wish I had pizzazz, then Dwight would look gaga at me."

Obviously surprised that these people might think like that, Bunny gazed at Tess's small eyes and mismatched features. "Maybe I can find time to show you some makeup tricks."

Tess's noisy gratitude finally cracked her facade. Alec quickly stepped in to the rescue. "Time to move on."

Outside the building, Bunny ripped the clip out and fluffed her hair again as if desperate to hide how badly the troop had shaken her. It seemed sad to see the warmth and gentleness disappear behind her glamour image. He wondered why she felt such an urgent need to hide behind a shield. "I wonder if a woman like you, with all your gifts and privileges, can understand how hard it is for exceptional people to fit into a normal world."

Frowning over painful thoughts, she gazed up at the cloudy sky for a moment, then looked levelly at Alec. "An accident of nature gave me an IQ at the top end of the spectrum, so I understand exactly how lonely your people feel in an average world."

And that answered his question as to why a gorgeous lady needed to erect a protective shield around herself. Feeling a rush of tenderness, he tossed out a probably hopeless invitation. "It's a nice spring day, and past lunchtime. Want to sit at a picnic table and share my sandwich?"

"I should get started on the report." Hesitating, Bunny studied him sidelong for a moment, snapping her gum, then she smiled. "Thank you, I'd like that. My stomach is hostile over not being fed before catching the plane this morning. Where's the table?"

He hadn't expected her to agree and pointed quickly past Manufacturing. "In that clump of pines near the river. Why don't you mosey on over, and I'll be with you in two minutes."

Rushing off before she could change her mind, he scrounged up some napkins and plastic glasses and grabbed his lunchbox. Laying a cloth on the table, he took out the sandwich, a banana, and a Baggie of brownies, and poured iced tea from his thermos. Seating Bunny on the wooden bench, he sat opposite her and blew out a breath. "Help yourself."

She'd been watching his actively grand service with fascinated eyes, and now she picked up half the sandwich. "What's in it?"

"Tuna with lots of chopped vegetables."

"That's my favorite." Putting her gum on a Baggie, she took a bite, closing her eyes to chew and savor. "Delicious! Did your wife make it?"

It took him a second to realize the fabulously beautiful ice maiden had asked if he was married. "Made it myself. Never had a wife," he said, wondering if she really was thinking of him along those lines. "Does your husband make your sandwiches?"

"Never eat 'em, too fattening. I shouldn't be eating this one." Taking another voracious bite, she chewed and swallowed, then said, "I've never been married either. A love affair with a computer keeps me too busy."

"A platonic relationship, I trust," he said, grinning over the notion of dedicated, desirable power women loving computers and giving birth to successes instead of babies. Watching her eat, he wondered if she'd go at sex with as greedy an appetite.

Then a tantalizing notion tickled his mind. The impossible dream. He'd long ago given up his chances for an involved relationship, believing maternal instinct was built into women. But was it in a dynamo like Bunny? He wasn't a solitary man by nature, and his enforced swinging-single life was lonely and meaningless. Maybe . . .

Feeling a sudden increased urgency to sell her on the Woodbox, he leaned forward. "Our blue-collar workers seemed to make you feel uncomfortable, Bunny. Why was that?"

She'd been watching a tug-drawn raft of logs on the river, but turned to scowl at Alec. "They were too eager to tell me about their jobs, too friendly. You must have primed them to butter me up, and I hate being manipulated."

He stared at her in surprise. "I didn't prime them,

that's how they always act. What kind of dog-eat-dog world do you live in?"

"I thrive on the fast track," Bunny said instantly, chin lifted in a challenge.

Alec brushed away a bug that had dropped out of the tree, wondering how to sell a fast-track woman on the snail's-pace Woodbox. "No track stars working here, just nice people, three fourths high-school graduates. . . ." He went through the statistics, ending with, "Most are married with children, and the rest wish they were."

Putting the last bite of sandwich into her mouth, she glanced at him and then away. "You too?"

He was too vulnerable to admit an impossible yearning for an unobtainable dream. "Nah, marriage isn't for me, I'm a freewheelin' kind of guy." He pushed the Baggie of brownies toward her. "Want one?"

"No, thanks, they're decadent." She pushed them back and put her gum in her mouth.

He felt childishly hurt, as if she'd rejected him. "I suppose all you eat are tofu and bean sprouts?"

"I'll bet my arteries are cleaner than yours," she said, and stood up. "Thanks for lunch, but now I have an urgent report to research." Lifting a high-heeled shoe over the picnic bench, she stopped astraddle, the leg of her jumpsuit snagged on a splinter. "Oh, no, I'm stuck."

"Don't move, I'll get it."

Alec came around the table and bent over to work the delicate fabric free. With his head inches away from her left hip, her perfume was penetrating his system, setting off a full range of hopelessly wishful desires. She shivered when his fingers tickled the back of her knee.

"Got it," he said, straightening up. The pink spots on her cheekbones and the heavy lids over her eyes told him she'd felt a response too. The idea was so exciting, it turned his tongue rash. "Are you a little confused about who you really are, Miz Bernice Fletcher?" A teasing grin lifted the corners of his mustache. "It seems to me you're just a Nerf ball under that killer hype."

"Don't ever underestimate the killer hype," she said in a terse voice, frosting him with frigid blue eyes. "And I despise being called Bernice!"

Alec watched her grab her briefcase and march away. Rapping himself on the head with a fist, he muttered, "Great going, Golightly! That's handling the campaign with real finesse."

Bunny rushed toward the main building. She hadn't intended to like Portland, but the blanket of silvery clouds hanging over her head, the hills, pine forests, and river were all very seductive. Pulling the door open, she glanced back toward the picnic table and Alec. Speaking of seductive, she couldn't figure out how a gadfly in a Hawaiian shirt could have thrown her so far off kilter.

After she'd spent a lifetime building an image to hide her feelings, how had he guessed she was floundering in an identity crisis? She seemed to have a gaping hole in her life, or perhaps it was an inner woman fighting bonds. Which was ridiculous when she had everything most people dream of: money, success, glamour. She'd had several lucrative job offers she couldn't motivate herself to accept. Compared with them, the Woodbox assignment was insignificant. So why did she feel the fate of real people resting on her shoulders like hot coals?

Marching into the building, she saw it as adding insult to injury that every time Alec Golightly had looked at her with those sea-green eyes, her fingers had twitched to snatch off her cursed new glasses. And she wasn't even vain; her appearance was simply a tool to accomplish what was expected of her.

Why? Sure, he had a good body, a sexy pirate's mustache, and a lovable face, but she'd been programmed to admire powerful men like her father. And sixteen plus eleven years with the factory added up to his being twenty-seven to her thirty-one, making her feel old. His flip remark about being partial to brilliant women had really lit her fuse. Men weren't! She knew that from bitter experience.

Slipping into the rest room and safely out of earshot, she burst out, "Damn. *Damn!*"

She froze when a toilet in one of the cubicles flushed. Nan Turner came out, straightening her dress over the mound of her pregnancy. "Something wrong?"

"No, it's just . . . nothing." Mortified over being caught in an unprecedented flare of emotion, she opened her briefcase and began freshening her makeup.

Nan fiddled with her own auburn hair, looking worried. "If that butterfly of an Alec got fresh, I hope it won't reflect on the job you're here to do."

Bunny smiled. "I believe getting fresh is called sexual harassment now, but there was none of that." She paused, then couldn't resist asking, "What do you mean by butterfly?"

"Well, nothing, just that he's a man to do more flirting than settling."

"I see." Holding her mouth open to apply mascara, Bunny wondered if Alec was one of the men who saw bedding glamorous women as a challenge; she'd been hurt by a couple before catching on. Not that it made any difference, since she wouldn't be there that long. Packing everything back in her briefcase, she said, "I've had the tour, now why don't you show me what *really* makes this factory run?"

"Glad to." Nan led the way to the business office and explained her computer system. "Use my desk, I'll take the table and the backup monitor. If you need anything, ask."

"Thanks, I will." Bunny sat down and looked at the homey touches around the desk. She picked up a picture. "Is this your family?"

Nan nodded proudly. "My husband, Chuck. He glues laminate here at the Woodbox. That's our daughter, Debra, and here's the second child, due in six weeks," she said, patting her front.

Bunny had no idea what having a baby or being part

of a family was like. Her mother had died when she was a toddler, and her father had always been more friend and business agent than Daddy. "Do you enjoy being a mother?" she asked.

Nan grinned. "Sure, even though the timing for a baby is bad, considering the situation at the Woodbox." She broke off. "I didn't mean to bore you with the sordid details."

"No, I really am interested," Bunny said, with more hot coals of involvement building up on her shoulders. "But I'd better get cracking on this report of mine."

TWO

Eight hours later, shoes kicked off, the glow of the monitor flickering on her face, Bunny was still sifting through data. Totally absorbed in the present operation and past history of the Woodbox, she didn't realize the windows were night black. The only sounds were the creaks of an unoccupied building and the steady snapping of her gum.

Succumbing to curiosity, she pulled up Alec Golightly's employment history. To her astonishment, he had a double degree: business and psychology. Leaning back in the chair, she stared at the screen, wondering why the man was wasting himself on a minimal job in a dying factory.

Bunny never daydreamed, but she was sapped after being on the go sixteen hours and eating practically nothing all day, and vulnerable to mind lapses. Rubbing one shoeless foot dreamily against the other, she imagined Alec kissing her mouth. Taking off her glasses, she pondered how his mustache might feel against her skin. . . . Soft? Bristly?

She gave a hearty yelp when her fantasy took on a voice. "Fascinating reading, huh?"

Swiveling around, she gaped at the devilish, sensual expression on Alec's rugged face. His other charms were nicely displayed as he straddled a chair, dressed in gray trousers, a white shirt open at the neck, and a navy jacket. "When did you come in?" she exclaimed, slapping her glasses back on.

"A few minutes ago," he drawled. "You were so fascinated with the monitor, you didn't notice." Noting the expression on her face, Alec tucked a teasing grin into the corners of his mustache. "I'm not one to interrupt research, especially if it might be about me."

Caught! There was nothing to do but brazen it out. "I've yet to meet a man more exciting than a computer. I was simply gathering information for my report."

He aimed a knowing smile at the monitor. "I would have spiffed up my records if I'd known you were going to use me for such lengthy gathering."

She quickly switched off the computer. "Your records are remarkably spiffy already. I can't help wondering why you haven't lived up to your potential."

"I'm just plain lazy, I guess," he said, giving a demonstrative shrug.

It seemed to Bunny there might be secrets hidden behind his shadowed eyes, but that didn't make laziness any less a sin in her estimation. "With your education, how can you be satisfied holding down a minor position in a dead-end factory?"

Gazing at the golden highlights cast on her hair by the flickering fluorescent light, Alec felt his way toward planting a seed in the mind underneath. "The factory isn't dead end unless you decree it so in your report." He paused. "And working with retarded people isn't wasting my talents."

"I can see it isn't. They touched me when I visited," she said gently, then leaned forward. "But you could make a major impact on the problems of retardation at a national level, maybe make a mark on the world." Frowning, she recognized *major impact* and *making a mark* as boosters her father had often used on her.

Alec smiled amiably, his eyes flinty green with determination. "I touch the lives of real people every day in my job." He let a pregnant pause stretch. "Can you say that about whatever you do for the consulting firm and Eleganté?"

"Touché," Bunny conceded, thoughtfully blowing a bubble.

Alec let out a breath, delighted to have made the first tiny inroad on his campaign to win her over. Better to back off before the next onslaught. "Okay, good, if we have that settled, let's get down to the important stuff. I guessed you were the type to burn the midnight wick, so I'm here to drag you away from the computer and out to dinner."

"Dinner?" Bunny repeated, leery of even a superficial short-term relationship with this very seductive butterfly of a man. Still, she *was* starving, and Alec did look more debonair than dangerous in a jacket. The night was a little scary outside the window, and she was far from home, lonely, and undecided about the future.

Catching herself in the act of taking her glasses off, she realized she was also ripe to be plucked. "Thanks, but I'm exhausted after being on the go since four this morning. I'll have room service at my hotel." She reached her arms toward the ceiling in a tired stretch. "And then to bed."

As he watched her breasts lift and her pelvis thrust forward in the arching of her svelte body, Alec's nerve endings went off like sparklers. His attraction to the sensual career woman was growing; the idea of something budding between them buzzed in his mind like a bee. Curious about her feelings on the subject of relationships, he asked, "Don't you ever get lonesome going to bed by yourself?"

Dropping her arms, she glanced at him. The green fire in his gaze lit secret places in her body. "I don't sleep around, if that's what you have in mind."

His lips curved in a smile. "Well, I can't say the concept hasn't entered my mind, in passing. Also in passing, I have a strong feeling it would be far more than just sleeping around with us. It'd be lovemaking."

Disgusted with herself for feeling so tempted to play flower to a talented butterfly with his sweet, sincere act,

Bunny said tartly, "*Love*making takes more time and commitment than two days, Golightly Man."

Considering that he had so much more in mind, it pleased him to have this modern woman flare back like an insulted virgin. "I can't argue with your logic," he murmured, letting his gaze play over her body. "But I'd sure like to." Cocking a finger at her, he got up and walked out.

Mouth agape, Bunny stared at the empty door. She couldn't believe he'd up and left because she wouldn't dish out sex. She hadn't felt so rejected since discovering boys didn't care to date brainy girls. She'd just about decided to advise Eleganté to keep the Woodbox and boot Alec Golightly when he came striding back in, his arms loaded. "What *are* you doing?" she exclaimed.

"I suspected you'd refuse my invitation to dinner, so I came prepared. Pizza, paper plates, a bottle of good rosé, real wineglasses," he counted off, unloading on the table. "Rats, I forgot forks. You'll have to use your fingers." Turning on a tape player, he filled the office with mellow jazz and held out his hands. "Come and eat."

Thrown completely off kilter by this baffling man, Bunny tossed her glasses on the desk and reached out to let him pull her to her feet. The sensation of his callused hands on her soft palms relit the fire in her body. Her voice sounded husky when she whispered, "I haven't eaten pizza in years, Alec. It's too fattening."

"I suspected you'd think that too." The musky scent of her perfume had invaded his system. Under the ceiling light, her hair was liquid amber, her eyes sky blue and glittering with sensuality. Pizza was the farthest thing from his mind, but at least she wasn't running away from the neutral topic. "So I ordered vegetarian . . . light cheese, thin crust . . . low-cal."

Without her shoes, Alec seemed taller. She had to tilt her head to gaze into his rough-hewn, so very seductive face. "Low-cal *pizza*?"

Smiling, he placed Bunny's hands flat on his chest so he could use his fingers to measure her waist. "Look at that, my fingers almost meet around your middle. There's nothing to you. The pizza won't make half a bulge."

"A bulge?" His racing heart and rigid nipples were separated from her palms only by shirt fabric. His eyes were hot jade. She couldn't take her eyes off his pink, tempting lips or stop herself from wondering how the pirate's mustache would feel against her skin.

A battle of sorts seemed to be going on behind his face, as if he thought he shouldn't kiss a visiting efficiency expert. Apparently he lost, because his head came slowly down. When his parted lips covered hers, she went wild over the erotic sensation of the fringe of hairs brushing her cheek, her upper lip, even her nose. For once, the reality was far more exotic than the fantasy.

Her head whirled when he ran his tongue along her lips. Legs melting, she clawed her fingers into fists on his shirt to support herself.

"Youch," he whispered against her mouth. "You're pulling chest hairs."

She stared into his eyes, then jerked her mouth away, uncurled her fingers, and tottered back. A second later the humor of it struck, and she burst into laughter.

"Shoot." Alec groaned, his breath coming in quick gasps. "Remind me to shave my chest next time."

"There won't be a next time, Golightly Man." Bunny backed farther away, refusing to contemplate his chest hair. The mustache was bad enough.

"Would you believe I didn't plan this?" he asked, running his hands through his hair.

"No." Slipping her glasses on, she laughed again. "I've heard of candy being dandy, and liquor being quicker, but pizza is . . . ?"

"Pizza is pizzazz, like you claim to be." Alec poured wine into two stemmed glasses and held one out.

She shook her head regretfully. "I do love wine, but I seldom drink anything alcoholic."

"What is this? You don't eat, you don't drink, no sex. What are you, a closet nun?" His personal charms didn't seem to be melting her, so he glanced around the business office, praying she'd begin to feel involved and interested enough in the factory to lengthen her stay. Then he, as an extension of it, would have time later to pursue his suit. "Come on, one glass. You deserve a toast for your work on the Woodbox."

Glancing at the worrisome research papers that had begun to indicate the factory wasn't all it could be, Bunny gave in. "You're right, I deserve a toast," she said, taking the glass. "I honestly hope the Woodbox will live long and prosper." A dimpled smile curved her lips. "And you, too, Golightly Man." Saluting him and then the computer, she took a hearty sip and closed her eyes to savor it.

Alec lifted his glass and sipped a toast for what had sounded almost like a positive attitude. "Could it be that old icy Bunny isn't as detached as she'd like everyone to think?"

Opening her eyes, she lifted an elegantly arched brow above a gold frame. "My killer hype may occasionally soften a bit, but never to the point of a Nerf ball."

Inwardly cursing himself for the present as well as his previous lamentable lapse, he said, "My apologies. I can't seem to control my mouth the way I should."

"I'll drink to that." Bunny took another gulp, then her smile sagged and she drooped with the exhaustion of a long, taxing day. "Unfortunately, old dependable, detached Bunny had better be back when I go home again."

"Good grief, I was only teasing. You mean you actually are softening toward us?" he said, seating her at the table. "Here I assumed it was the wishful thinking of a pretty ordinary Woodbox guy around a glamour queen."

"Oh pooh, you aren't ordinary by any stretch of the imagination." Startled to hear something so trite roll off her cautious tongue, Bunny suddenly realized she felt very relaxed and loose now that the first sips of wine had hit her empty stomach. She even laughed and said,

"I'm not a glamour queen. It's an image to hide the fact that I'm a nerd."

"Why hide it?" Alec asked earnestly, since a lovely lady nerd seemed the very thing he needed to mesh with his barren life.

Bunny shrugged lightly. "Glamorous people are more likely to succeed."

He rubbed the back of his neck. "Why is the fast track and success so important to you?"

Bunny studied his face, brought to a halt by something she'd never considered. "What else is there? Success has always been my top priority. Was. Will be again, as soon as I decide in what direction I want to aim my life." Dropping the frustrating subject, she sniffed the aroma of the flat box. "The dietary pizza is getting cold."

Smarting over having his campaign slide back to square one, Alec lifted a slice to her plate, delicately breaking the cheese tethers with his fingertips. Then he watched her sink her teeth in and close her eyes to chew and savor. "For someone with a phobia against fattening food, you certainly do enjoy the simple act of eating, don't you?"

Opening her eyes, Bunny sipped her wine and laughed. "If I spent any longer than two days around you and your food fetish, I'd go home looking like a potbellied pig."

"I've heard they're very sweet and lovable." Gazing at her plump, moving lips, he felt an urge to nibble, suck, and feed on her mouth with his tongue. His self-imposed taboo on flirting was becoming damned restrictive. Picking up a slice of pizza, he took a bite and tried to get his campaign back on track. "What do you think of the Woodbox after poking around the records?"

Holding out her glass for a refill, she smiled. "I haven't unearthed any gunrunning, drug smuggling, or embezzlements, but I don't want to commit myself until I've looked through everything."

Alec finished off the last bite of his pizza. "So, then, what's life in southern California like? I've been dying to ask since you first arrived, is your house furnished in Swedish modern?"

Wiping her lips with a napkin, she had to admit somewhat sheepishly, "I still live with my father, and he isn't the simple Swedish type."

"Bunny, the daddy's girl?"

The wine had filtered up from her empty stomach to swirl around her brain. Before she could warn herself to be careful, she blurted out something she'd never realized bothered her. "George isn't the daddy type, and I've never been a girl."

"I can relate to that, since I never had a chance to be a boy either." Balancing his chair on two legs, Alec braced a knee on the table and bit into a piece of pizza, gazing at her silk jumpsuit. "But I'd risk a bet you can afford a house, maybe even two of your own. What's holding you back?"

Bunny smiled at a fine thread of cheese draped over the side of his mustache. "Running a company like Wilderness Enterprises was so stressful and demanding, I didn't even have time to spend my salary, much less buy a house and put down roots. My computer was my best friend and my only lover. It was my entire life, and now that it's been phased out, I don't seem to know who I am any longer."

"I'm not surprised." Alec nodded, pleased she trusted him enough to talk about her troubles and worries. "How'd you land a plum like Wilderness Enterprises?"

"I didn't land it, I created it. I went to college with the nature photographer. I was twenty-one when I began building the Enterprise around him. Nick."

Her smile faded when she thought of the dark, handsome, dynamic man who'd seen her only as a buddy, not a woman. Nibbling the pizza away, she held up the bare crust, all she seemed to end up with in life. "Nick used to call these pizza bones."

The same yearnings Alec often felt were reflected in her face, as if this lovely, complete woman had been lonely, too, longing, wishing for someone in her life. He felt an almost uncontrollable urge to hold and comfort her. "You loved Nick, didn't you?" he said softly, bringing his chair down on four legs.

Bunny quickly sipped wine and tried to wave off her most painful secret. "It was one of those things that flare up, then fizzle into a friendship, sort of." But her unruly tongue went ahead and blabbed the worst. "The reason Nick sold the Enterprise was so he could move to Montana and marry another woman."

Warm with compassion, he reached out and circled her wrist with his fingers. "It must have broken your heart to lose both at the same time."

To have her eyes fill with tears was too much to tolerate. Jerking free, she lifted her glass in a toast to herself. "Don't you worry about me. I've had offers from other film companies. I'll be perfectly all right as soon as I go home and pick one out of a hat."

Alec nodded and tossed in a suggestion. "Or maybe something simple and relaxing would do you good. Like being, oh, say, the general manager of a homey little factory."

"You mean, like, oh, say, because you're in trouble and you want to bring in the heavy artillery?" Giving a short laugh, Bunny thought she understood why he was working so hard to romance her.

"It's more than that," Alec said, too unsure of himself and her yet to explain exactly what. "There's something to be said about an intimate little job, working with people who really care about you."

"Yes, I suppose." Cocking her head to the side, Bunny considered the idea rather wistfully. "But I've been groomed from childhood to climb high up the success ladder. People are counting on me to fulfill my potential." Sighing, she took a swallow of wine. "Now let's talk about you. What do you think, dream, and hope? Where do you live?"

"Me?" Alec threw his crumpled napkin on his plate, thinking it wouldn't benefit the campaign to reveal too much about himself and the thoughts he'd been thinking since she appeared on the scene. "I live in the state of Washington."

Bunny puckered her forehead in a frown. "Isn't that unhandy when you work in Oregon?"

"It's pronounced Or-y-gun, unless you want to sound like a tourist," he said, grinning. "My Washington house is just across the river from the Woodbox, less than a mile as the crow flies, maybe twenty by bridge."

She cocked her head at him. "Furnished in Swedish, or from kits?"

"Traitorous as it sounds, no kits." He reached for the bottle to fill their glasses. "My mother decorated for me and furnished the house in contemporary, or something."

Biting back a yawn, Bunny felt more relaxed than she'd ever felt before. "She live with you?"

"No, in Seattle, and I'm not as interested in the house as I am in a boat I'm building in my backyard."

"Motorboat, dinghy—what kind of boat?"

"A sloop. An oceangoing thirty-two-foot job with a single mast."

Widening her eyes, she blinked when she saw two of him. "Good Lord! How do you plan on getting it to water?"

Alec scratched one side of his drooping mustache. "I'll figure something out when the time comes."

"Uh-*huh*. If you should happen to get thish—" Her tongue wasn't working any better than her eyes, so she took pains to enunciate. "If you get this vessel launched, where are you planning to sail?"

Leaning back, he propped one ankle over the other knee, half-embarrassed over another of his impossible dreams. "I don't know, somewhere beyond the blue horizon."

"Soun's romantic," she murmured, delicately covering a yawn. "Though somewhat 'morphous."

"So amorphous it'll probably never happen," he said, sighing. "Where would you go, if you had the whole world free and open to you?"

Bunny had never had time to dream about freedom and drifting. "I'd shail—sail down the Los Angeles to the coast and get on with my life, I guess."

After trying to decipher that, Alec glanced at her and muttered, "Whoops."

Clapping a hand over a yawn that threatened to split her face asunder, Bunny said, "I better go fin' my bed." Rising unsteadily to her feet, she grabbed the back of the chair and turned to peer owlishly at him. "It's very hard to believe, but I think I'm drunk. And I only had two glashes of wine."

"Two and a half, Princess." Laughing softly, he came around the table and put his arms around her. "Come on,

I was the one who made this tactical campaign error, so I'll see that you get safely home. What hotel?"

Sagging against him, she simply couldn't hold her eyes open. "Can't remember. Key'sh inna briefcase."

Alec carried Bunny out into the foggy night. It seemed so achingly sweet to have her delicate weight curled against his body, her arms wound around his neck, and her face nestled in his shoulder. The dream crystallized in his mind; one way or another, he meant to have this sophisticated, gentle, dynamic, sweet, complex woman in his arms for real.

She was limply asleep before he'd buckled her into the passenger seat of her red sports car. She didn't even moan when he picked her out again and carried her into the hotel, up the elevator, and into her fourth-floor room.

Laying her on the queen-size bed, he folded her glasses on the table. The jumpsuit looked expensive and he thought she'd want to take it off. "Rise and shine, pretty lady," he called softly, shaking her. "Bunny, wake up!"

No response.

"Oh, hell, what the heck?" Unbelting and unbuttoning, Alec found stripping a one-piecer off limbs as limp as cooked spaghetti to be a major task. Tossing the suit on a chair and the panty hose on the floor, he blew out a frazzled breath. Looking down at her, he couldn't seem to draw another breath in.

After flitting around women all his adult life, Alec

had seen his share of nude female bodies, but never one so streamlined. Sculpted into sensual curves by sleek muscles, she didn't have an ounce of cellulite under satiny skin that glowed with a mocha tan. Her breasts were small and firm, nipples like raspberries showing through the blue lace of her bra. Below her taut waist was a cunning navel. He couldn't stop his gaze from flitting downward to the triangle of blue hiding a dark secret between her legs.

Groaning over the urges tormenting his body, Alec tossed the other side of the spread over temptation. He put her keys in plain sight on the dresser and reset the alarm; she seemed like a seven o'clock riser. If he'd had any sense, he would have left it at that, but Bunny looked so sweet and innocent, he couldn't resist leaning over to brush her lips with a good-night, sweet-dreams kiss.

It threw him off balance when her eyes popped open. Still perfectly unconscious, perhaps acting out a dream, she licked her lips, gave a throaty laugh, and brushed a fingertip across the edge of his mustache.

Then she opened both arms and reached out to him.

THREE

Bunny was still twenty leagues deep in slumber when the alarm buzzed. Groaning, she pried her eyes open and slammed it into silence. Her first realization was that her mouth tasted like a rotten avocado, her next, that the room was filled with morning light. Grabbing her glasses, she peered at the clock. She'd overslept by two hours, and she couldn't even remember resetting the alarm. The last thing she remembered was eating pizza and being . . . *drunk*?

Swinging her legs out of bed, she came face-to-face with her jumpsuit, crumpled over the back of a chair, panty hose rolled in a donut on the floor. Her clothes were a professional investment; even drunk, she wouldn't have thrown them around. The alternative hit her like a dash of ice water. *Alec.*

If hot and randy Alec had undressed her, then . . . ? She looked down at herself. No, surely he couldn't have done *that* without her knowing. Could he? "Damn butter-flies!" She'd always prided herself on knowing exactly what she was doing at all times, and why. She'd end up in a madhouse if she didn't finish her research and go home this very day.

Dashing in and out of the shower, Bunny set out to build an image like a fort. After shaping her hair into a spiraled mass and putting on an extra complement of makeup, she dressed in a starkly tailored brown suit and a high-necked cream silk blouse. All she needed was her briefcase, but her constant companion wasn't in the room. It seemed a miracle her keys were on the dresser. Grabbing them, she rushed out the door.

For anyone walking into the Woodbox business office, the evidence of last night's orgy was there for all the world to see: two plates, two glasses, and an empty wine bottle. Nan was at the table, feeding her pregnancy by nibbling cold pizza. "I took you for an earlier bird than this," she said, flicking a curious but discreet glance at the peacock-blue shoes under the desk. "Guess you musta had a late night. Help yourself to coffee in the file room."

Steaming cup in hand, Bunny found her briefcase and research notes on the desk, undisturbed. The uncertainty of whether she herself had been undisturbed induced her to gnaw a piece of pizza. Had he or hadn't he? And how could she look him in the face if he had the nerve to turn up here?

Throwing the crust down, she exclaimed, "I have to get this job *done*!" Taking off her jacket, she rolled up her sleeves and sat at the desk. Then she moaned as she remembered a promise. "I told Tess I'd show her some makeup tricks. How am I going to fit that in?"

Nan got up to throw the rest of the pizza and the empty bottle into the waste can. "If you let it slide, she'll probably forget you offered."

"But I wouldn't. No, it'd haunt me if I disappointed her. In fact, I should include the other girls, too, so they don't feel left out." Reaching for her briefcase, she began to get up. "I'd better go buy makeup for them."

Nan waved her down, smiling. "If you can be so nice, the least I can do is run out and buy what you need. I'll bring the girls here at lunch break."

Gratefully Bunny crawled into the sanctuary of the computer, and the morning sped by. By noon Alec hadn't put in an appearance, which to her mind proved by default that he felt too guilty to face her. After the four women of his special troop filed into the office, she was too busy for the next hour to worry about him.

She'd seldom dealt with even normal people on a personal level and felt ill at ease at first. It passed as soon as she saw that they felt downright frightened. One of the women wouldn't say a thing, another shyly answered her questions in monosyllables, a third only hummed. Tess functioned approximately on the level of a ten-year-old and made up for the rest with an excited running commentary.

It delighted Bunny to win them over with nothing more than smiles, gentle talk, and the touch of her hands. To her surprise she found it unexpectedly fulfilling to see their faces bloom with color, laughter, and a smidgen more self-respect. She felt an unfamiliar emotion, a melting compassion, as if an extinct volcano were erupting in her heart. The strange sense of having a shackled woman inside grew stronger.

When they filed out again to go back to Packaging, she was dying to tag along and see if Dwight would look "gaga" at Tess. But she couldn't bring herself to risk running into Alec. Besides, her deadline was approaching, so she had to rebury herself in computer printouts.

It was midafternoon, after Nan had left the office for a break, when Alec finally turned up. She swiveled around, and there he was in a yellow-and-orange Hawaiian shirt and snug jeans, straddling a chair. His grin was as innocent as an altar boy's, but that didn't prove anything, because his eyes looked worried. "Where'd you come from?" she asked, toying with a pen.

"I've been out and about, spending the morning at a Special Olympics workshop. When I came back, I found tulips blooming in Packaging. Tess had been flouncing around Dwight until he was so bedazzled, he steam-wrapped his hand in with a bookcase. The Woodbox needs more of you, spreading glamour like a contagious disease."

Impatient with idle chatter, Bunny went for the meat of the matter. "What happened last night—*exactly*?"

A rather nervous glint of laughter in his green eyes suggested Alec knew what was bothering her. A brief struggle seemed to go on behind his face over whether to give a straight answer. He folded his arms over the back of the chair and lifted both brows. "I'm sorry to say you got potched. I had to carry you to your car. Great car, by the way. Is it yours?"

She threw the pen down on the desk. "It's a rental! Will you just tell me what happened?"

He peered contemplatively at the ceiling. "Let's see, I drove you to your hotel, carried you to your room, and laid you on your bed."

"Then you left," she said hopefully.

"Not exactly." His mustache twitched. "Your outfit wouldn't have survived a night of tossing, so I helped you out of it."

Sinking lower in her chair, she hated thinking she'd ceded entire control of herself to him. "Then you left?"

"As I recall, that's when I kissed you good night, and you tickled my mustache," he said, nodding. "And held out your arms, just as inviting."

"Oh, dear God." She moaned, tightening her arms over her chest to keep her heart from plummeting to the floor.

"*That's* when I left, before I did something we'd both regret." Alec scowled at her. "Did you think I had myself a quickie without you knowing, Miz Fletcher? Let me go on record as saying I'd no more take advantage of a defenseless woman than bomb an orphanage."

Throwing her glasses on the desk, Bunny pressed her hands over her face, melting with relief, furious with herself, and utterly humiliated. "I can't believe I got into a situation where I had to suspect such a thing! *Me* of all people!"

It didn't help when he laughed. "Fact of the matter, you were so hot and sexy, stone-cold sober, it would have been anticlimactic to settle for an unconscious spaghetti woman. Bringing in the wine wasn't a very smart move on my part."

Bunny dropped her hands and shook her head. "I can't believe I acted like such a fool. *Me!*"

"You did not act like a fool!" Swinging his chair around, Alec sat frontward, looking at her with serious, tender eyes. "You acted like what you were, Bunny, a stressed, exhausted, perfectly innocent woman. When you said you weren't used to drinking, I shouldn't have pushed wine on you." He measured a quarter inch with his thumb and forefinger. "I was the one who came this far from making a fool of myself. You were so lovely, so vulnerable, leaving was the hardest thing I've ever done."

Bunny gazed meltingly into his eyes, a meeting of warm blue sky and tumultuous green sea. "I am very lucky it was you, Alec, and not a lot of other men I know. I think you must be a saint."

"Oh, no, I'm sure not one of those." Leaning forward, he cupped his hands around her cheeks. "I very definitely want to make love to you, Princess. But when I do, I want you wide-awake, participating, and begging for more."

Her body went soft and tingly over the thought. "I wish there'd been more time," she said softly, gazing at the pink lips under his mustache, at his sensual eyes, at the broad shoulders under his wild shirt. "Now I'll always wonder what might have happened between us."

"Why wonder?" he whispered, pushing his fingers into her hair. "The Woodbox needs you, I need you, Princess. Stay and let's explore the possibilities."

His flawed, disappointing offer caused an inner stirring in Bunny again, the imprisoned inner woman fighting her bonds. But the humming computer was louder. It was like an alter ego reminding her she was in the business office of a ragtag factory, face-to-face with a butterfly who wanted her to save them from disaster. Withdrawing from his tempting hands, she put her glasses back on. "I'm not cut out for the Woodbox, and there isn't time to explore you, Golightly Man. I'm catching a plane home in a few hours."

"Already?" With time rapidly running out for his impossible dream, he glanced rather desperately at the printouts scattered around the computer. "Didn't you find anything at all you liked about . . . the Woodbox?"

Bunny frowned unhappily, thinking about the women from the special troop. "I found lots I liked, but unfortunately the factory is only minimally productive, wages are on the low side of national averages. From what I could tell, I believe the factory might have had potential if the previous parent company had been more aggressive with the marketing. If I put a lot of work and some serious creativity into my report, it's possible I can convince Eleganté to do that. The special troop is very definitely a selling card."

Alec felt as if he might melt with relief; he had a feeling nothing or no one would stand in Bunny's way if she set out to accomplish something. It delighted him even more to see involvement on her face. But he needed *time* to talk her into taking the Woodbox on, being there, day in and day out, so he could also sell her on a relationship that'd fit both their unique needs.

Scrabbling for some way to keep her, he came up with a brainstorm. "Tell you what, to demonstrate my total faith in your capabilities, I'm going to throw a gratitude party. Tonight, at my place." He jumped up and made for the door. "See you there, Princess."

"Alec, I can't come to a party!" she called after him. "I'm catching a place at eight."

He popped his head back in with a determined grin. "After accusing me of violating your inert body, the least you can do is stay one more day and see my boat."

"That's not fair," she protested. But he'd already ducked out. "I'm not going," she said to the computer. "I'd be a fool if I let this thing go any farther."

⸎————⸎

At six that evening Bunny drove across the bridge into Washington State, then eastward on the wooded ridge along the Columbia River. "Good Lord!" she exclaimed when she located Alec's house. It was a sprawling graystone, a veritable mansion with two wings slanting in from the main body and a mossy shake roof. Nestled in a grove of dense evergreens, it had a breathtaking view of the Columbia River and Mt. Hood. The grounds were lushly landscaped with rose gardens, a tennis court, and a cottage. Apparently she and Alec didn't come from such different backgrounds as she'd thought.

Parking with several other visiting cars, she walked up on the porch to knock the brass knocker on the dark red carved door. Within seconds the lord of the manor threw it open. "I'm happy to see you, Princess," Alec said softly. "I was worried you wouldn't come."

"You were so pushy, I almost didn't," Bunny said, soaking up the look of him to remember after they parted. His shoulders were very broad under a striped soccer shirt, his legs strong and virile in white shorts. It seemed odd after being around Hollywood-handsome men to find his rugged, gentle face so utterly adorable. "I'm glad I changed my mind."

"I'm glad you're glad." He stood poised, as if he wanted to take her into his arms, but she drew back a step, wrapping her arms around herself, leery of taking chances. He shoved his hands in his pockets instead. "Come in, I suppose we'd better go find the others."

Alec escorted her down the hallway toward the back

of the house. Consumed with curiosity, she peered into the large, gracefully decorated rooms. "You said your mother helped you decorate in 'contemporary or something,' but this is more like gorgeous! How on earth can you afford a house like this on a department head's salary?"

His grin was sassy under his mustache, but his eyes were shadowed with secrets. "My fairy godfather tapped me with a wand and said, 'Let there be glitz.' "

"You call this glitz!" she exclaimed, looking in the living room. The furniture and colors were strong, earthy, and comfortable, the walls decorated with seascapes and colorful Northwest Native American art. The windows brought the view of the river and the mountains inside. A native-stone fireplace filled an entire corner. She turned to lift a brow at Alec. "I have a feeling this house is wasted on you."

"Yeah, I guess it is," he admitted in an oddly sad voice. "But you'd fit into it like a velvet hand in a satin glove, Princess, judging by your outfit." He let his gaze flow down over her black denim gold-studded jacket, the matching skirt stretched like skin from waist to midthigh. Her sandals were gold, too, and her camisole top was the exact blue of her eyes. "Is that a little old rag out of *Vogue*?"

Flustered by the heat in his gaze, Bunny laughed. "A little old rag I picked up on Rodeo Drive."

He'd kept the house he had no love for as an ace up his sleeve to interest her, but she'd trumped it with

Rodeo Drive. Sighing, he said, "We'd better go find the others."

Bunny stood in the French doors, looking out at a vast flagstone terrace with padded lounge chairs and a group of some twelve partying people. The swimming pool was Olympic size, and a barbecue pit was spreading a tantalizing aroma of sizzling ribs. The boat dominated everything, supported by scaffolding, the hull gleaming with white paint and black decorative stripes, the prow jutting out high above.

"I thought you were kidding when you said you were building an oceangoing ship in your backyard!" she said, glancing back at Alec. "What possessed you to tackle such an enormous job?"

Pleased she was interested and impressed, he breathed out a laugh. "Maybe there's a little killer hype under my Smurf-ball exterior."

Bunny thought it might be highly interesting if what he said was true, but obviously he was only teasing. "How long have you been working on it?"

"Going on four years. The outside is finished, but there's lots of work to do on the interior yet."

Impatient calls pulled them out on the patio. Henry and his wife, Nan and Chuck, along with the other department heads and spouses welcomed Bunny so warmly, she felt instantly at ease.

Tending the barbecue, Alec was tickled to watch her, stretching out in a lounger, laughing at earthy jokes from the men and listening with interest to the wives giggling over the perils of juggling homes, husbands, children, and jobs.

Nan was the reigning queen with her pregnancy, the other women inquiring about her progress, eager to share their own pregnancy-and-birth experiences. Bunny listened with the fascination of a woman being introduced to a new world. Just a tiny bit, she began to regret that babies and husbands hadn't been programmed into her schedule. It might have been fun to be a member of the sorority.

After dark, when she had finished eating ribs and trimmings and cautiously drinking a glass of wine, Alec held out his hand. "These guys can take care of themselves now, let's go for a walk."

Relieved to escape her budding but impossible yearnings, she put her hand in his without hesitation. "I'd love to."

Strolling across the grass, they left the terrace and the lights behind. The sky was black, with patchy clouds drifting over a three-quarter moon. City lights sparkled across the river. The western breeze smelled faintly of the ocean and strongly of the pine forest. Alec put his arm around her, drawing her closer to the heat of his body. Bunny found it very natural to curl her arm around his waist.

With party talk and laughter tinkling behind them, he debated what facet of the Woodbox might be most likely to induce her to stay with him. "You've made some friends at the factory, Princess. They like you."

"Do you really think so?" she said wistfully; friends had been rare in her regimented life. "I don't have much in common with them."

"Being nice to my girls is enough in common to win them over."

Bunny frowned thoughtfully. "I wasn't being nice, I think maybe I got more out of it than they did. I'm not sure why."

Alec nodded. "Eternal children, so needy, with so much to give if only we took time out of our 'superior' lives to recognize it."

She smiled at him. "They're lucky to have you for a champion."

"I consider myself the lucky one." Things were getting too personal now, so he changed the subject, murmuring impishly, "Too bad Nan didn't pass on the news that you apparently went home barefoot last night, leaving your shoes under the desk. The employees would have loved that."

"I'll just bet they would have," she said, giving him a poke in the ribs. "I imagine you supply them with plenty of juicy gossip all by yourself."

He gave a burdened sigh. "It's a dirty job, but someone has to entertain the rank and file."

Wondering if he really did take his love relationships so casually, Bunny watched the lights of an isolated boat passing on the river. It reminded her of how lonely she was at times, how rare true lovers and close friends had been in her pressured life. "I wish I could have spent more time here and gotten to know everyone better, especially your very special troop." Glancing at his face, barely visible in the night, she smiled. "And you, of course."

His heart surged with yearning. "Don't go, Bunny. Stay."

"Stay and do what?" She felt that stirring again, an inner part of herself fighting to get out of a dungeon. It was scary enough to send a shiver through her.

Alec enfolded her in his arms. "Stay and make love to me, Princess." Sliding his hands up under the back of her jacket, he laughed softly. "You want me, too, don't try to say you don't. Stay and we'll make love the whole night long."

Curling her arms around his neck, Bunny looked into his face, made handsome by the shadows. Her breasts tingled, her body ached with need, pressed against his rugged male form. Her life was so empty, but a few minutes of uncommitted sexual release could never fill the void. Not even if the butterfly pretended he loved her, as they so often did with the greatest finesse. How many women had Alec pretended for, how many more to come? Did she want to be fodder for juicy gossip?

Lifting her head, she searched his face, frustrated by all her inner chain rattling. "I don't think one night with a man like you would ever be enough."

Curving his arms further around her slight body, he ached to offer her the world or the universe. Flawed as he felt himself to be, he was afraid to risk his heart.

Feathering kisses around her face, he took only a very cautious step into vulnerable territory. "I've got lots of nights, Princess. I need you. *The Woodbox does.* Make your home here. Stay."

Going stiff against him, she absorbed what he'd said. Then she pulled free of his arms. "Alec Golightly, are you actually trying to seduce me into saving the Woodbox?"

Stepping back, he felt unreasonably rejected because he'd been using the Woodbox to seduce her for himself. "I wasn't thinking about furniture kits just now," he said, hiding his disappointment and hurt. "But since you brought it up, let me bring it right out into the open. Yes, I'd like to have you stay and take over the Woodbox."

Bunny drew in upon herself. "Alec, I would have refused to run the Woodbox even if I weren't absolutely furious with you! I do truly sympathize with you and your employees' problems, but I can't help you out. I've got my own life to rebuild. Besides, you can't begin to afford the fees I charge."

Nothing she said was a surprise to Alec. Frustration and disappointment, not wisdom, led him to say, "You can't blame me for trying. Too bad the glamour Bunny turned out to be a nice lady. You'd be easier to forget if you were just a desirable body."

The words hit Bunny like a slap. Folding her arms over her ribs, she retorted, "Things would certainly have been a lot easier for me, too, if I hadn't run into a damn butterfly I liked!"

He folded his arms over his chest, biceps bulging. "Well, Miz Bernice Fletcher, you sure as hell have a funny way of showing that you like me."

"Where did you get the idea I should go to bed with you to prove I like you!"

"That isn't what I meant!"

"Then what did you mean?"

His throat tightened, stopping him from telling her the truth. "I don't know."

Hands shaking, Bunny took several deep breaths for control. "I don't know why we're making such a big deal out of this. We live at opposite ends of the coast, so it was only a fluke that we came together in the first place. And we obviously weren't meant for each other, you being who you are, and me being who I am. So that's that."

"I guess it is, isn't it?" he agreed unhappily.

The wishes quivering in the pine-scented air between them were too nebulous to be spoken. Bunny gazed at him a moment, picking at the gold studs on her jacket. "I guess I'd better go back to my hotel now. I have a very early flight to catch tomorrow morning. Maybe you'd say good-bye to everyone for me."

Alec had to stiffen his body to keep from reaching out to her. "Good luck with the big beautiful life you have waiting in southern California."

"Good luck to you, too, Golightly Man."

After watching the lovely, graceful woman walk away and disappear in the dark, he rubbed his hands over his face. He'd let himself hope, and now he felt emptier than ever before. It was as if Bunny had carried his last chance for happiness away with her.

He'd been a fool to dream about a loving touch from an untouchable goddess.

FOUR

Bunny walked into her father's Beverly Hills house the next morning, feeling as if her life would never be the same again. In two short days the special troop had touched her deeply. And she'd liked the other Woodbox people too. Their simple joy in marriage and motherhood had set her cursed shackled inner woman to fighting like an uprising slave. And *Alec*. How could she erase the sweet look of his rugged face from her mind? She hated thinking he'd seen her only as a challenge or as a solution to his Woodbox problems.

Dropping her garment bag and briefcase, she went to the living room. She'd always found solace in the familiar pearl-gray carpeting, French furniture in shades of blue, and the Van Gogh, artfully lighted against subdued wallpaper. In a glass case were mementos from her father's years in promotion: pictures of actors he'd built into stars, relics from major movies.

Moments later the man himself walked into the room in an impeccable gray suit with a color-coordinated shirt and tie. As always, George was the epitome of cool equanimity. She'd tried to duplicate his cool in her own life. "How nice to have you back, pet," he said, taking her into his arms.

"Oh, yes, I need a hug." Bunny pressed her face into his shoulder, wishing he could solve her current upheaval the way he'd soothed her *ouchies* when she was a child.

He settled himself on the blue-patterned love seat and patted the place beside him. "Come, sit down and tell me all about Oregon."

"It's Or-y-gun, George." She told him about the problems of the Woodbox and how much the people had affected her. But she avoided any mention of Alec, knowing her father would scorn a man in a stagnating position. Falling silent, she wondered if she might enjoy managing a tiny factory. It could be stimulating to convince Eleganté to keep it alive, then use some creativity in building it up and . . .

Imagining her father's opinion about *kit furniture*, she sighed, then smiled wryly. "My experience at the Woodbox was very interesting, but it didn't help me figure out what to be when I grow up."

George smiled with more than a little subdued excitement. "I believe your dilemma may be over. A new voice has entered the running. Faline Morris would like you to contact her."

Bunny's chin dropped. "You mean Faline Morris, who produced *Winsome Cloud*?"

"Yes, *Winsome Cloud* and several other highly acclaimed films with women's themes. She'd like you to call for an appointment."

Two days later Bunny hitched her rose crepe suit skirt up to perch on the vast walnut desk in George's high-rise office. "Now I can say I've done lunch with Faline Morris."

"Wonderful," he said, leaning forward. "How did she hear about you?"

"Preston Mann, the producer of Nick's movie, told her how well I did for him. She needs an associate producer, so she checked my entire history. Nick, bless him, gave me a triple A-plus." As she studied her manicured nails it occurred to Bunny that her hurt over Nick had faded like a mosquito bite, thanks to being preoccupied with Alec and a fresh new pain. "Anyhow, Faline would like to try me out, and if I prove myself, I can shoot up along with her success."

Her unflappable father gleefully threw a pile of papers in the air. "Shoot up to a position of power in the film industry? Perhaps buy into her business, or even become a producer in your own right? Bunny, my pet, this is what we've been working toward ever since you taught yourself to read at three." He eyed her. "You accepted, of course?"

Clasping her hands on her thigh, she frowned. "I told her I'd think about it. But, please, don't get upset, we have another appointment, day after tomorrow. I can't make a decision like that with the Woodbox report preying on my mind. The least I can do for those special people is devote my full concentration to their problems."

Picking up her briefcase, Bunny walked across the oyster carpeting in her father's elegant office, wondering how it might feel to sit in Henry's dumpy hole-in-the-wall. To see Alec every day. Watch him flutter his butterfly wings from flower to flower . . .

"Faline's offer is a dream come true," George said when she reached the door. "You mustn't turn your back on an opportunity that might occur only once in your lifetime."

Glancing back, she nodded thoughtfully. "Yes, you're absolutely right."

Three of Alec's employees were absent that day, and he was angrily banging screws around himself, hoping all Bunny's damn dreams were coming true. Because she'd starred in his fantasies, waking and sleeping, for two weeks since she left; it felt like a hundred years. A sad statement, when the woman had treated him to a soul-smarting rejection.

He'd been going around in a murderous mood, furious with her, himself, and everyone else ever since. It didn't appease him to be rushing to finish out a late shipment. It topped all when the boss wanted to see him immediately.

Mustache bristling, Alec stomped into the main office. "This had better be good because—" His stomach dropped when he saw Henry slouched behind his desk, looking ten years older than he had the day before. "What's up?"

"Eleganté is closing us down. We've got three months to satisfy our current orders and phase the employees out."

Stunned, Alec stood in front of the desk. "But Bunny said she could convince them we had potential."

"Looks as if she didn't succeed."

Stuffing his lavender-flowered shirt down in his jeans, he pictured himself telling thirteen trusting, adoring retarded people that they were being thrown out on the street. He smashed his fist down on the desk in helpless frustration. "Her Majesty must have been too busy with her high-powered life to worry about our little problems." He glared at Henry. "You aren't going to take this lying down. You're going to fight 'em."

Henry rubbed his bald pate. "It worked with Goliath, but I'm no David. But if you took the job over . . . ?"

Alec walked to the window and gazed out. He'd refused the promotion before, thinking the special troop needed him there with them. Now they needed their jobs more. He wished he could have talked Bunny into taking the job. At least he wouldn't have felt so alone. Unfortunately the Academy Award–winning actress had bigger roles to star in than the Woodbox. "Okay, dammit," he said, squaring his shoulders. "Tell the board they can vote me in as general manager."

Henry got up and came around the desk. "They already have, so there's the boss seat for you."

Realizing he'd been had, Alec grumpily sat down behind the desk. Something came over him as he swung the swivel chair back and forth: a sense of power. A grim smile budded on his face. "Henry, we're going to give 'em hell."

"You can. I'm going fishing."

For three days Alec barely slept, dishing himself up a crash course in management techniques and Woodbox finances, hoping to turn up a simple solution, but there wasn't one. The prospect of announcing the threatened closure to the rank and file gave him the chills. Taking off his suit jacket and jerking his tie loose, he propped a hip on the windowsill, wishing his boat were finished so he could sail into the wild blue yonder, away from all his troubles.

As he idly watched a black Beemer with a bike mounted on top roll into the parking lot, it occurred to him that the cloud cover was as thick as it had been the day Bunny had arrived. His anger resurged when he wondered if she might have neglected the report as an ingenious way to punish him for making a bid for a relationship. Hurt to the quick and blaming himself now, he scowled at a woman getting out of the black car. She was very slender in a pants suit made of some cream-colored fabric, wearing jewelry in a rainbow of color, carrying a briefcase.

Coming to, Alec suddenly realized who he was watching. "What in hell does she want?"

Utterly exhausted after only two short naps during her two-day drive up from southern California, Bunny plodded across the parking lot. The gentle forested hills, blanketing clouds, and the eternal power of the river lent her a peaceful sense of reassurance—much needed reassurance, since she was still shaken over George's unprecedented eruption of disapproval.

Inside the main building, she bypassed the secretary and plodded through the office door. "I came as soon as I heard Eleganté was planning to—"

A tingle of excited surprise nipped her sentence off in the middle when she saw Alec, not Henry, sitting behind the desk. His lusty mustache, sea-green eyes, and the crisp brown hair falling over his forehead were the same, but his bearing had changed in a most exciting way. He looked authoritative in a gray suit, white shirt, and blue-patterned tie. She pushed her glasses up on top of her head. "What are you doing in here?"

"I belong here, so let me ask you the same question." He wished she didn't look so damn beautiful, taunting him with what he couldn't have. Answering his own question, he growled out, "I didn't realize how fast the vultures would gather to gloat and pick our bones after the kill."

Bunny stared at him a moment, then slammed her glasses back on. Red spots burned in her cheeks. "Vultures? What are you talking about?"

Alec stood up and leaned his knuckles on the desk. The hurts, worries, and fears he'd been stifling spewed out. "It doesn't matter that I fell for your flirty games and got hurt. I can understand why you felt you couldn't stay and help us, since I didn't ask very tactfully. But couldn't you at least have taken time out of your fast-track career schedule to write a decent report? If you thought you had to get back at me, let me say our employees deserved better!"

"I am not a *vulture* and I am not vindictive! I couldn't sleep nights, thinking about your special people." Digging in her briefcase, Bunny threw a folder on the desk. "There's the *excellent* report I wrote. They wouldn't look at it. Eleganté had already decided kit furniture didn't fit their image." Bracing her knuckles on the desk, she thrust her face toward his. "If you had the brains of a gnat, you would have known I'd do my best, you—"

Her added pithy expletive snapped Alec back to his senses. "You're right, it takes gnat brains to think you'd come way up here just to gloat. I—"

But she was off and running, not listening. "I did not play flirty games with you! It was the other way around. You and your wine and your *mustache*!"

Alec winced, knowing she was right. "Bunny, I—"

"I'm bone-tired after driving like a maniac to come up here." She blinked her burning, exhausted blue eyes and fought a trembling lip. "And my father almost had apoplexy because I put a spectacular career offer on hold so I could try to help you solve your stupid crisis!"

"All I can say is I'm sorry," Alec said miserably. "I dreamed up some misconceptions about you because things have been very tense around here. But I guess that's no excuse."

On her knuckles, nose to nose with him, she felt her uncharacteristic flare of anger evaporate as fast as it had erupted. She was so tired and so stressed, his sad-eyed expression of remorse struck her as inexplicably funny. Despite her effort to control it, laughter bubbled up in her throat and pealed out into the room.

It didn't surprise Alec that she'd succumbed to hysteria after the things he'd said to her. What to do about it was the mystery. Leaning forward, he kissed the dimpled corner of her mouth. The cure was instantaneous. Her laughter stopped as if he'd cut it off with the touch of his mustache. When her eyes turned heavy with desire, he couldn't resist running his tongue along the velvety line between her lips.

Shocked back to her senses, Bunny jerked away as if she'd been burned. "Darn you, Alec Golightly, I swore I wasn't going to fall for any of your games this time!" she exclaimed, rubbing her cheek with a shaking hand.

When her fingers came away black with wet mascara, she fled to the rest room. It took her twenty minutes to pin down her effervescent emotions, reestablish her image, and stride back into the office, snapping fresh gum.

Alec was waiting contritely behind his desk. "I'd like to apologize for false accusations and for calling you a vulture."

"I should hope you would," Bunny said, breathing out a laugh. "And I'd like to apologize for throwing a tantrum. I have never acted that way in my entire life! I don't know what there is about you that causes all my emotions to go critical."

"*All* your emotions?" His mustache curved up in a wistful grin. "That's an interesting thought."

Looking at him, Bunny had to cautiously agree. He looked forceful, even with his jacket unbuttoned, his tie jerked loose, and a tinge of passion lingering on his rough-hewn face. To her, power was a very erotic attribute in a man. "Be that as it may," she reminded herself, "I only came back to help you work out your crisis. If you need me."

Leaning back in his chair, Alec spread his arms wide. "I need you, want you, desire you. You can have the position of general manager, as of right now, if that's what you want."

Giving a laugh, Bunny raised her hand. "No, that's not why I came back. But can you use an adviser?"

"You betcha!" He gazed longingly at her face. "How long can you stay?"

"I understand Eleganté has given you three months, so that's my max," she said, then lowered her brows. "If I'm going to stay, I want us to be up-front this time so there aren't any misunderstandings. I'm not permanent and you're, as I recall, a freewheelin' kind of guy, so this is a working relationship only."

"Mmmm." Alec found Bunny Fletcher especially desirable when she acted authoritative, and he wasn't about to make any promises.

Content she'd made her point, she delicately twitched up her cream pant legs and sat down on the chair in front of his desk. "What happened to Henry?"

"He retired and went fishing. I'm boss now, amusing as you may find that."

"I don't find it a bit amusing. As I recall, I railed at you for wasting your potential. I can tell by the look in your eyes and that pugnacious chin that you'll make a good executive." She laughed when he stuck out his chin a little farther and mimed a solid right with a fist. "What have you done so far about the impending closure?"

Blowing out a harried breath, he smoothed his mustache with the pad of a thumb. "A corporate lawyer is helping me with the procedure for an employee buyout. Hopefully Eleganté will agree to sell and carry us for x number of years until we can pay them off."

"Leverage is a solution I thought of too," Bunny murmured, playing with the colorful chunky jewelry clustered on her chest.

Clasping his hands behind his head, Alec frowned at the ceiling. "Somehow I have to convince the employees to throw enough money into the pot for a down payment. I haven't told the rank and file what's going on yet. I'm planning to announce the crisis tomorrow morning and lay the plan out."

Bunny felt a rush of sympathy, realizing how much he cared for the Woodbox people. "That's going to be really emotional, isn't it?"

"You betcha," he said, sighing. "And besides that, they may not want to risk their nest eggs in a chancy venture, and I wouldn't blame them when they're looking at unemployment. So a buyout might not be possible."

"Yes, I see." Taking off her glasses to rub her tired eyes, Bunny wished she knew how to turn a butterfly's interests toward commitment with nice, instinctive womanly talents. All she had to offer was her business acumen, and he didn't seem to need that. "You've already thought of everything I would have suggested, so apparently my gallop to the rescue was premature. I guess I might as well trundle back home again."

"Good Lord, you can't be thinking of leaving again!" Alec exclaimed, his heart sinking over the thought of her going away without exploring their possibilities. "I may have ideas, but I don't know how to fine-tune them. And

PR! No one would hand money over to me when I have the tact of a rabid skunk."

"Or a vulture," she murmured, giving a laugh because she did have something he wanted and needed after all. "All right, I'll stay and lend you my services. My *business* services, that is. Gratis, since I doubt the Woodbox can afford me."

Leaning his elbows on the desk, Alec studied her with puckish green eyes. "Tell me, Miz Bernice Fletcher," he said, deviously devising a plan to tie her down, "what would you do if someone with your smarts walked in with so generous an offer? Would you give them free rein without spelling things out, signed, sealed, and official?"

"Not in your wildest dreams, Golightly Man," she declared instantly, delighted that he knew better than to trust unwisely. "Okay, I'll work out a contract that satisfies us both. If I become a temporary employee, I can take my fee in shares and sell them back to you when things are rosier. How would that be?"

A grin hatched under his mustache and his body began tingling with anticipation. "Since we're spelling things out, there is one point I want to make. You forfeited your chance to take over as general manager, so that means I'm in charge. I make the final decisions. Do you think you can live with that?"

She laughed. "I'll do my best to remember you're the boss and I'm only an adviser. But it might be wise to write a gag order into the contract."

Giving a deep sigh over things going so well at long last, Alec leaned back in his chair and gazed curiously at her. Happy as it made him, it seemed odd a woman with her business potential would give up a chunk of her life for a little old factory like the Woodbox. "Why'd your father have apoplexy over your coming here?"

Bunny slipped her glasses up on top of her head and got up, twitching her sharply creased pants up to sit on the edge of his desk, one leg wound around the other. "It had to do with my receiving a job offer anyone in my business would kill for. Do you know who Faline Morris is?"

"Faline Productions?" He gave a low whistle, his optimism sagging. "Seems like I asked this when you first came, but what in hell are you doing in a place like this?"

"My father's point exactly," she admitted wryly. "But I discussed it with Faline, and your special troop captured her imagination. She agreed that I could come here before giving a final yes or no to her offer. George had a fit anyway." Frowning, she twisted a ring with a large purple stone around her middle finger. "I hated to upset him like that. My mother died when I was two, and he's always been so sweet to me. We're very close."

Alec nodded, rocking his chair. "My father . . . well, I lost him when I was nine, so my mother and I have been closer than most too."

"Really?" Bunny said, glancing up. "Then we have something in common after all. A similar history."

"It looks like it," he mused, rubbing the scar cutting across his chin like a misguided cleft. "But there's still a gap as wide as a canyon between us if you're going to work for Faline."

Frowning, Bunny blew a dismal bubble and popped it in her mouth, then shrugged. "I don't see how I can refuse her offer. It's a dream come true." A thought popped up out of the empty inner gap, almost as loud as an impatient spoken voice: *Whose dream?* It startled her into jumping off the desk. "I'm so exhausted I'm goofy!" she exclaimed. "I'd better go find a hotel and a bed."

Alec got up and shoved his hands in his pockets, jacket pushed back from his chest. Now that he had her safely pinned down to the Woodbox, he could concentrate on campaigning for himself. "You can stay at my place for the duration if you want to."

Feeling a rush of excitement, Bunny quickly slipped her gold-framed glasses back on. "Oh, I can live with you, can I? How handy."

"It was a perfectly innocent offer," Alec vowed, an out-and-out lie. "I have a little guest cottage, separate from the house. You can stay there and have as much privacy as you decide you want."

The arrow of a thrill shooting through her body was an indication of how much privacy she was likely to want. She'd be a fool to accept, but the need for a quick night's sleep made her gullible. "I'm game to give it a try."

Alec blew out a relieved breath. "You're just one

damn surprise after another, Miz Bernice Fletcher," he said. "I expected you to tell me where to go jump."

Popping a bubble in her mouth, she pinned him with an icy blue gaze. "If you intend to call me Bernice, I'll tell you exactly where to jump, and how deep."

"Bunny, I meant Bunny."

FIVE

Aching to rest her eyes and body, Bunny dogged Alec's tire tracks across the bridge and eastward back up the north side of the river in her black Beemer.

She found it odd that he was driving a blue Mustang convertible. Almost as odd as a man with his education limiting his career the way he had. It was a step up for him to be the manager. Though the chances for the Woodbox were not good, he'd have had a taste of power by the time it went down. Perhaps he'd want to move up to something more important, and she had the business expertise to help him develop into . . .

The thought of Alec on the fast track was depressing, so she dropped that trend of thought. Truth be told, she'd been pushed beyond her limits all her life, spurred to achieve success. She didn't know how to slow down. It seemed sad to think of the easygoing Golightly Man harnessing himself to that kind of situation.

When they arrived, his house was another mystery: still enormous, the boat still unfinished in the backyard, and the grounds still spectacular. Even on a manager's salary, he'd need a "fairy godfather" to afford it. Outgoing and open as he acted, his life was a series of blank pages to her.

Alec led Bunny into the small living room of the cottage. Looking around at the dusty covers over the furniture, cloudy windows, and corners festooned with cobwebs, he scratched his cheek and lifted his brows. "I guess I was a little premature in offering you the use of this place. I didn't realize it'd be in such musty shape. You can't stay here until I have it cleaned."

Barely listening to him, she found herself captivated. The cottage reminded her of a cozy little dollhouse, not that she'd ever played with dolls. Gazing out the window at a view of forested foothills, majestic Mt. Hood, and the broad Columbia River, she felt a sense of seclusion and serenity. She imagined her spinning inner dynamo might slow and relax here. "If I dust up the bedroom a little, I can stay the night." She added rashly, "And I'll clean up the rest of the house myself too. Later."

Alec skeptically eyed her expensive pants suit and regal bearing. "I'll bet you've never cleaned a house in your life. Go on, admit it."

Bunny didn't feel disposed to reveal that George insisted mundane chores were beneath her talents, and there'd always been a housekeeper to do for her. "I have an educated mind, so I'm certain I can figure out how to clean a little bitsy house."

"I'm sure the brilliantly educated can bore themselves by doing housework as well as anyone, but why bother?" he said, not eager to see the dedicated career woman who so appealed to him develop domestic interests. "Come and stay in the big house tonight. I'll have someone swamp the spiders out of this place tomorrow."

"Alec, I am staying here tonight," Bunny said, setting her chin.

Feeling a faint rumble of some future complication, he had no choice but to give in. "If you're dead set, I guess I'd better bring some sheets and towels." Walking to the door, he looked back and listed a full complement of cleaning supplies, hoping to dampen her domestic aspirations. "I'll also bring rags, mops, brooms, scrub brushes, a vacuum cleaner, and cleaning solutions."

After he'd gone laughing on his way, Bunny prowled through the small rooms, yawning and fastidiously protecting her cream pants and blouse from dust and grime. At the end of the tour she realized that aside from throwing the windows open for fresh air, she had not the vaguest idea how to apply the cleaning tools he'd mentioned.

Alec returned wearing white shorts and a blue T-shirt, giving her an interesting view of his vigorously masculine body. Discreetly covering her yawns, she watched intently as he whisked away the dust with vacuum-cleaner attachments. "I don't know why you think I can't do that."

"I don't know why you think you want to," he said, plumping the pillows and smoothing a patchwork comforter onto the bed. Surveying the finished product, he was very aware of the svelte and sexy Bunny readily available on the other side of the bed. Thinking taboo thoughts, he wondered if he could relax his flirting restrictions now.

Glancing at her, he noticed that she was too tired, even if she were agreeable. "It probably isn't a very good idea to hang around the bed, Bunny Lady."

Lips parted, she let her eyes roam wistfully over his sensual face and vigorously masculine shape, then gave her gum a loud snap and beelined for the door. "Right, this is a business relationship. I'm going to bring my things in."

Pleased over her obvious attraction, Alec followed Bunny out and grinned at her little black Beemer. "Is that giant, mutated mantis attacking your car?"

"Don't make fun of my racing bike," she said, laughing. "I don't usually have the time or patience for aerobics or running, so I bike to work." Popping the trunk lid, she bent over and reached in for a suitcase. "It keeps me in shape."

"It certainly does," Alec murmured, studying the rear of her svelte length before moving her aside and taking over the heavy work. "But my place is at least twenty miles from the Woodbox, too far for biking."

"That's just an easy practice jaunt," she murmured, watching his muscles bulge as he lifted a huge suitcase out of the trunk.

"Do you always rush around like a rat on a tread-mill?"

"I thrive on the fast track," she said by rote, though she was so tired, the thought brought tears to her eyes.

Lifting her professional wardrobe off a rod in the backseat and carrying them inside, Bunny hung each piece meticulously in the closet. When Alec brought the last of her boxes in, they stood in the bedroom, gazing at each other. Awareness of the bed and each other was written on both their faces. "How about having dinner with me?" Alec asked softly.

She yawned again, clapping a hand over her face. "I'm too tired to eat."

Reluctant to leave her delectable company and go back to his big, empty house, Alec lingered when he knew he should leave. "Sure you won't be scared, staying here by yourself?"

The warmth in his face told Bunny he'd take her in his arms and love her thoroughly if she gave him the slightest encouragement. It scared her to want it so badly. "I'd have more to worry about if I weren't by myself, Golightly Man." Her grin stretched into a huge yawn.

Cupping a hand around her cheek, he touched his lips to hers. "Okay, Princess, I'll leave you in peace if that's what you want."

After he'd left, Bunny pressed fingertips to her lips, wishing she did know what she wanted. *Yes*, she wanted to open up and love Alec, be loved, but she was afraid of being hurt. Coming to the Woodbox and meeting real people had caused her to wonder about marriage, and even babies. But she didn't know if she had what it took to be a supportive, loving mate and mother. And how could she fit them in with Faline and the dream come true?

Throwing herself on the bed, she cried out, *"I don't want to be superwoman any longer!"*

Next thing Bunny knew it was morning. Popping to a sitting position, still fully dressed, she peered at faded, floral wallpaper and cloudy light streaming through dusty plantation shutters. Surely she hadn't actually cried herself to sleep over being a bright, successful woman? Alec inspired the most bizarre behavior in her!

Realizing he'd probably left for work hours ago, she rushed through her morning routine, shaped her hair into a spiraled mass, and tugged on a suit of fluorescent lime and black spandex tights and biking shirt. Folding her office clothes in a backpack, she hurried out the front door.

A cardboard box was sitting in front of the door, a scrawled note taped to the top:

Morning, Sleeping Beauty.
You need fuel in your tank to pedal twenty miles.
  Alec.

Grumbling about never eating breakfast and his being a bad influence, she sat on the step and ate half a cantaloupe, two prewarmed sausages, and a bagel with cream cheese. After sipping a second cup of coffee from a thermos, she unwrapped a stick of gum, took down her bike, and zoomed to the Woodbox.

Hanging her helmet on a handlebar, Bunny found the main building deserted. With a stab of guilt, she remembered Alec had said he would be announcing the Eleganté decision to the employees this morning. And she'd overslept, leaving him to face it alone.

Sprinting across the grounds, she popped into the cafeteria. The employees were all there, sitting at tables, whispering anxiously among themselves. The special troop was clustered in a far corner, gazing around with their unsuspecting eyes, grinning as if they'd been invited to a party.

Alec looked very alone, wearing a tweed jacket, a shirt and tie, and a morbid expression. Some of the tension eased from his face when she slipped up beside him. "Am I ever glad you're here. I've been feeling very isolated." A glance at the bright spandex hugging her body brought an anemic smile to his lips. "Are you trying to give us men a heart attack?"

"You men have better things than me to worry about."

"Right." Running his hand over his hair, he said, "The gang's all here, so I might as well get it over with."

"Thumbs up," Bunny whispered, and watched him walk to the front of the room.

The assembly sat in shocked silence when he talked about the Eleganté decision to close the factory and described an employee buyout. After he'd listed the risks as well as the possibilities, they acted as if everything was his fault, lobbing inflammatory, belligerent questions at him. The emotions were so raw, the special troop became agitated and caused such a ruckus that the new head of Packaging had to take them out.

Alec's face was pale and beaded with perspiration by the time the questions petered out. "All I'm asking is that you think about a buyout," he pleaded. "In two days we'll vote on whether to go for it."

Gathering his papers, he walked with stiff-necked dignity out of the cafeteria.

Following, Bunny felt her heart go out to him. She wanted desperately to comfort him, but she wasn't sure how, or even if he'd accept it after having his ego shattered.

Seeking solace in his own way, he said, "I'd better go talk to my packaging troop. They didn't understand a word I said. All they knew was something dreadful is happening."

They found the kit-assembling room ticking like a time bomb. The majority of the troop were rattling hardware and bickering, defying the department head and the supervisors trying to settle them. Three were wailing at the tops of their voices, begging to go home.

"Jake's ready to blow," Alec said. "See what you can do with the others while I calm him down."

Dealing with emotions was very far out of Bunny's field of expertise. Half-afraid she might make things worse, she could do no more than hand out hugs and smiles. "I'm so happy I'm back with you again."

Fortunately the novelty of her brilliantly spandexed presence distracted them. Unfortunately Dwight, the brain of the bunch, refused to leave well enough alone. "What did the Golightly Man talk about back there?" he demanded. "He say we don't do a good enough job?"

"No, you do a fantastic job, all of you." With their eyes fixed on her face, Bunny propped a hip on a table and tried to describe the crisis in terms that they could understand. Content that they were following, she ended up with, "The Golightly Man said the employees can buy the factory and own it themselves. Anyone who invests—pays money—can own a piece of the Woodbox. Sort of."

After running the concept through the slow-moving channels of his mind, Dwight tugged a wallet out of his rear pocket and threw a bill on the table. "I want the piece with my shrink-wrap machine."

"No, wait, that isn't how things work!" Bunny said, holding the bill out toward him.

With eyes only for *his* shrink-wrap machine, Dwight was finished with listening. The others aped their peer leader, tossing crumpled bills and change on the table. Face bright with some startling makeup variations, Tess threw her two bits in, beaming. "You and the Golightly Man going to see we okay, hah?"

Within minutes the room was calm, with business as usual. Jake had settled down to counting screws, so Alec walked up to aim a humorless laugh at the pile of money. "I should have let you give the spiel in the cafeteria."

"Don't joke about it." Bunny groaned. "How am I going to convince them to take their money back?"

He scraped the bills and coins off the table into a screw pail and handed it to her. "If they own a piece of the action for a while, they'll have something to remember after they find out I can't do miracles."

Outside Packaging, he scrubbed his hands over his face, drained and demoralized. "The rank and file didn't go for my buyout, so I guess this is the end of the Woodbox. How am I going to tell my troop that life as they know it is over?"

Weeping inside, Bunny plodded beside him toward the main building. "Someone said it isn't over till it's over. Let's wait and see how the vote goes."

"False hope," he muttered. False hope to feel so comforted by having Bunny walk in step with him. There'd been many times in his solitary life when he had ached to have someone of his own to share the ups and downs. If the Woodbox went under, she'd go back to her own life.

In his office, Alec perched on the windowsill and stared at the fogbound hills. The sky was heavily overcast and spitting rain, matching his mood. "If I had my boat finished, I could have . . ."

Bunny felt like weeping over the sadness in his face and voice. Stepping close, she pressed her front against his side and wrapped her arms around his shoulders. "What would you do if you had your boat finished?"

"Nothing, I guess." Curling his arms around her waist, Alec pressed his face into her shoulder. He melted into the solace offered by the gentle woman who so seldom emerged from behind the glamour shield. "It's just that the rank and file have been my friends for eleven years, and it hurt to have them turn on me the way they did in the cafeteria. I wanted to play superman and promise those people everything would be all right."

Bunny tightened her arms and rested her cheek on his crisp brown hair. "You were honest, that's better than superman. Personally I can't understand why they didn't buy the idea. You were charismatic enough to talk a boulder into moving. You even had me fired up."

"If I had to be a one-spark man, I'm glad it was you I kindled. Actually I kindled one single flame and thirteen sputters from the troop."

As he smiled wryly Alec's mustache sparked a shiver in Bunny when it brushed the creamy skin in the V-neck of her biking top. Her response reminded him he was holding a sensual, lovely woman in his arms. Her perfume was musky, with a hint of clean feminine sweat. Touching his tongue to the salty valley between her breasts, he could almost forget that the rest of his life was lying in rubble around his feet.

The moist touch tingled on Bunny's skin and sent a spear of desire flying into the soft areas of her body. Uncurling her arms, she put a hand on either side of his head, turning his face up. "I believe you've recovered your randy good spirits, Golightly Man."

He let his hands move slowly down over her lime-green hips. "No, I still feel really, really sad." Pretending to joke, he ventured into vulnerable territory. "It doesn't look as if we'll have a business relationship much longer. We'll have to think of another name for the relationship."

"You're playing with butterfly words now." Kissing him lightly on the mouth, she walked away and sat on a chair in front of the desk, unwrapping a fresh stick of sugar-free gum.

Feeling rejected, Alec jerked his tie loose and undid two buttons of his shirt. Walking to the desk, he poked a finger through the money in the screw pail. Giving a short laugh, he sat down behind the desk. "Sixteen dollars and twenty-four cents. I'm not going to be sitting in the chair of very minor power for very long."

Crossing her knees with a swish of spandex, Bunny gazed at him. Now that he'd had a taste of management, would he be interested in going on to bigger and better things? What might that mean for them? "What'll you do if the Woodbox doesn't make it?"

Clasping his hands behind his head, he gazed

through the window at the blanket of threatening clouds. "I've never thought about working anywhere but the Woodbox."

She nodded intensely. "That's why I've been at loose ends. I thought the Enterprise was forever and hadn't plotted alternative objectives. Every career experience should lead to other, equally exciting new ventures."

Hands still clasped behind his head, he moved his eyes to look at her, mustache curving up. "You must be quoting your father again. If you're suggesting I run like a racing rat on the fast track, forget it. I'd rather get a shopping cart and go for homeless."

"Well, I happen to enjoy challenge and competition. And I think you do, too, if you'd be honest with yourself."

Alec's smile faded. "Bunny, even if that were true, I couldn't leave now. My special troop will need me more than ever, with things going to hell the way they are."

He jumped when his secretary's voice blared through the intercom. "Alec, are you there? Your department heads want to see you."

An increasingly pregnant Nan led the pack, followed by the three men. Jack Budd, head of Maintenance, acted as spokesman. "Our people didn't need a couple days to think, Alec. They talked everything over in the cafeteria and voted. It's unanimous."

He winced as his stomach took a plunge. "I didn't expect doomsday quite so soon. But since I couldn't guarantee success, I'm not surprised people with mort-gages and families don't want to gamble."

Jack pushed his hard hat up to scratch his head. "I dunno what you're talkin' about. They were mad and raving at first, but after they'd got that out of their systems, they discussed your deal. Everyone is fired up and gung ho to fight for the Woodbox. Almost everyone wrote out IOUs, pledgin' how much they could throw in the pot for the down payment when you get things mapped out." He held up a sheaf of folded notes. "Where do you want 'em?"

Alec stared at them with disbelief. Bunny gave a triumphant laugh and jumped up to grab the screw pail. "Put them in here with the previous contributions."

Stuffing the IOUs in, Jack winked at her spandex. "Glad you're on our side, ma'am. A man might have trouble gettin' tough with you in a business deal."

She winked back. "Then let's hope it's a man I come up against at Eleganté and not another woman."

After the department heads filed out of the office, Bunny skipped around to sit on the desk, a leg on either side of the Alec's knees. Grasping his shoulders, she gave him a shake. "Wake up and congratulate yourself! You have pulled off a brilliant coup."

Coming to life, he took a long, slow glance at the slender body displayed so tantalizingly in front of him. A grin spreading over his face, he dragged her into his lap and wrapped his arms around her. "Damn right I did, Princess."

Extracting her arms from his tight embrace, Bunny clapped both hands on his cheeks. "Didn't I tell you you had charisma?"

"I didn't catch the message before," Alec murmured, pursing his lips teasingly. "Think you could find another, better way to get it across?"

"I might be able to." Tossing her glasses on the desk, she threw her arms around his neck. Burying her mouth in his swashbuckling mustache, she parted her lips in an invitation.

In a tempting preview of the bigger act to come, Alec entered her mouth with his tongue, tasting and searching. His swelling response had the force of an ocean tide. Her body was as lithe and sinuous as a jungle cat's, molded to his from lips to thighs. His breath came in gasps as he kissed her cheeks, her eyelids, nipped her earlobes with his teeth. "Princess . . . Oh, Lord, I've wanted to kiss you and hold you like this ever since you came back. You taste good, smell good, feel so good in my arms."

"Alec, I shouldn't—" she began, but couldn't speak over the tripping of her heart when he brushed her lips with his mustache. Flares of desire raged from his hands, gliding over the spandexed sweep of her back, inflaming every quivering nerve in her body. "We shouldn't be doing this," she whispered halfheartedly.

He moved his hand ever so slowly up her thigh to trace the joining of thigh to pelvis. "If you don't want me, all you have to do is get up."

"Yes . . . I'll get up," she whispered, burying her face in the curve of his neck.

"But you don't want to, do you?" he whispered, probing two fingers lower. "You want me here, don't you, Princess?"

"No, I . . . yes!" she cried out when he caressed the pulsing area at the base of her body. Losing all will to resist, she let him lay her back onto the desk, head among the papers, knees bent over the edge.

Marauding her mouth with his tongue, Alec rubbed trembling hands over the spandex on her breasts, her stomach, down over her body, ending the trail of fire on the eager pulsing area between her legs.

Straightening up, he braced a hand on either side of her body and looked down, searing her face with the green fire in his eyes. "I want to make love to you so badly, Princess," he whispered in a husky voice. "You're so incredibly beautiful, a sex goddess."

"Sex goddess?" Bunny whispered, going still and cold. She couldn't bear to think he was making love to the glamorous image she'd created, not the real her. Pushing him away, she struggled up off the desk and moved out of reach. "My fault. I shouldn't have let things go this far."

Alec stared at her a moment, then dropped back into his chair and rubbed his hands over his face, wondering how he could have pranced right into a position where he could be rejected again. "Why didn't you slap me in the face and be done with it? The least you can do is tell me what went wrong."

Putting her glasses on, her body still throbbing with need, Bunny paced restlessly, miserably around the office. "Nothing went wrong! The problem is, everything was too right. If you'd been any other man, I might have gone through with it."

"Oh, well, thanks a lot," he muttered. "That makes me feel worlds better."

Stopping in front of his desk, Bunny speared him with angry ice-blue eyes. "How do you suppose *I* feel about you seeing me as a sex goddess? I have no intention of letting you make love to me for some kind of trophy on your shelf."

Flushing with resentment and hurt, Alec shoved his hands in his pockets and stalked across the room to glower out the window. "If all I'd wanted was a trophy, you know damn well I've already had a perfect chance to have you."

"Well, I don't think you have any better idea about who I am inside now than when I was asleep."

Alec turned his head, ready to lash out, then thought better of it, realizing she was right. He had been seeing her only as what he needed in his life: a brilliant, hard-driving career woman. What about that gentle inner core she kept hidden from pain? "You're right, I don't really know you. But you don't know a hell of a lot about me either."

"That is my point exactly, strangers have no business making love." Leaning her hips on the desk, she gazed at his lovely broad-shouldered form and sweet, rugged face. "If we're going to fall into these situations, maybe I shouldn't live at your place. It'll make things very hard."

The notion of her leaving chilled Alec; it'd happen too soon anyway. Leaving the window, he propped a hip on the desk next to her. "Don't move out, Bunny, please. I'm not attracted just for sex, or because you're so beautiful."

She gazed intently at him with molten blue eyes, wanting to believe. "Then why, Alec?"

Breaking out in a sweat, he swallowed through a dry throat. "Because I've begun to feel deep feelings about you." He blew out a harried breath. "Think there's any chance for us if we get beyond being strangers?"

"Oh, Alec, I really hope so," she whispered without hesitation. "But we have to be very open with each other."

"It's a deal." He raised three fingers. "I promise, seduction is taboo until you say the time is ripe."

Eyeing his puckish, sensual face, she laughed softly. "I have a feeling it'd work better if we both keep very busy getting a proposal ready to present to Eleganté."

SIX

"For strangers, we're absolutely terrific together," Alec murmured, his eyes glowing triumphantly as he cupped Bunny's cheeks between his hands. "You were fantastic, Princess."

"It wasn't me that was fantastic, it was you," she whispered. Sighing with equal satisfaction, she moved her face and kissed the hard palm of his hand. "I suspected you'd be good, but I never guessed you knew the right moves as if you'd been born to them."

"You inspired me," he said modestly. "By wearing that awesome outfit."

"This little old French designer rag I threw on?" she said, holding out her arms, briefcase in hand. She'd worn her good-luck suit to the appointment, a coral Chanel with a black band around the neck and down the two sides of the jacket, black jewelry and heels, her hair upswept in a sophisticated style.

Side by side they stepped into the elevator outside the sixteenth-floor corporate offices of Eleganté Furniture. After the doors slid shut, she looked Alec over. "Speaking of awesome, I haven't seen that suit before."

"Just a little old rag that I had especially tailored for this monumental occasion," he said, grinning as he held his arms out, briefcase in hand, to show off an utterly elegant charcoal-gray suit with faint pinstripes, complete with vest and maroon tie. His hair had been styled, his mustache neatly trimmed.

Poking the lobby button, she gave an exultant laugh. "We two power-togged individuals bowled over a half-dozen VPs and a board of directors."

"Did we ever, and here it is only just past noon. I thought it'd take all day, at least. I fully expected them to listen to our proposal, let us hang a few weeks, then turn us down. But they agreed, and I feel as if the weight of the world just lifted off my shoulders."

"Yes, me too." Bunny beamed happily. "Now we're going to be the proud owners of the Woodbox."

Alec went soft with anticipation over hearing her talk so possessively about the factory. Tilting his mustache teasingly, he said, "The Eleganté board was all male and that may have had something to do with our remarkably rapid success. You melted them like plastic."

"I've always said a little PR never hurts," she said slyly. "So let's not be sneering about pizzazz and the fast track."

Watching her elegant, lithesome shape exit the elevator, Alec murmured, "I'm not a man to sneer at pizzazz. Uh-uh!"

"Well, good." She tucked her arm through his as they walked across the lobby. "I had the expertise in finances and marketing, but you knew the factory inside and out, with an answer to every technical question at your fingertips. We make a fantastic team."

"You betcha!" he said, crowding into one section of the revolving door with her.

With his front brushing her back, he wondered if he could begin lifting his restrictions on flirting. Of course they still hadn't talked much about themselves or their feelings, but she'd begun saying *we* and *our* about the factory. Every day she stayed, she was becoming more involved with the employees. He figured once she was hooked on them, she wouldn't be likely to pack up and leave after the crisis passed.

"I personally won't feel secure about the deal until I see the terms spelled out," Bunny said, frowning as they walked outside. "If things sound too good to be true, they usually are."

Knees canting out, ambling beside her across the parking lot, Alec glanced up at the murky Los Angeles midday sunshine beating down on his head. "I personally am more worried about the smog corroding my teeth, Miz Fletcher."

"Surely you wouldn't trust air you can't see!" Giving a hoot of laughter, she opened the door and got in behind the wheel of their rental car.

Taking off his jacket, vest, and tie, Alec climbed into the passenger seat. He rolled up his sleeves to midforearm, preparing himself for some serious campaign strategy. "Our plane reservations aren't until late tonight, so let's celebrate by doing something really fabulous and special. How about Disneyland?"

Bunny cocked a condescending blue eye at him. "Is that the best you can come up with? I didn't even go to that rinky-dink, tinsel-town place as a child, and I'm not about to begin now."

Donning an expression of horror, he demanded, "How can you say something so sacrilegious? If you've never been, I have an overwhelming urge to take you and watch your eyes bug with wonder. In fact, I consider it my solemn duty to see that you experience the magic."

Bunny couldn't help laughing. "Don't be ridiculous, Golightly Man. I am too old for that kind of foolishness."

Grinning, Alec tweaked a ringlet of hair hanging in front of her ear. "How old are you anyhow? You've never told me."

"None of your business," she shot back. His being four years younger than she was one area where they'd remain strangers forever, if she had her way. "Disneyland is for kids."

"Well, pretty lady, I happen to be a great big kid yet," he drawled, running a finger down her neck, making a brief foray into the scooped neck of the black blouse under her jacket. At her shiver, he withdrew his finger, content to have lit a desire. "Come on, loosen up and take a chance."

Tightening her fists on the steering wheel, Bunny fought against wanting to feel more of his touch. The shackled inner woman was complicating things by begging her to run free and play hooky from her regimented life. "Maybe up in Portland you can talk me into doing crazy things, but not here in my own territory."

Exasperated, Alec lowered his brows. "Your childhood must have been even more deprived than mine if you grew up thinking like such a stick. When I was a kid, we didn't have two nickels to rub together half the time, but my mother scratched up money to take me to Disneyland. I'll bet you don't even know how to have fun."

Glancing at him in surprise, she realized she *was* acting like a stick. And also that he'd just given her a glimpse into a past that had left him with a flattened nose, a scarred chin, and a fear of revealing his feelings. Her defenses crumbled. "All right, I'll go," she said softly, then made a face at him. "But I'm not going to have fun."

Arriving by freeway, Bunny took off her jacket, hoping her blouse and coral skirt wouldn't end up ruined. Going all the way, she put her glasses in her briefcase and locked both in the trunk.

Putting his arm around her shoulders, Alec walked her through the turnstile. "Okay, Princess, settle back and pay attention. Old Alec is going to give you a crash course in Fun 101."

❖━━━━━━━❖

The sun was sinking toward the west, silhouetting the gently waving palm trees, before Alec walked Bunny back out of the gates again. Sunburned, tired, sticky from junk food and drinks, she felt as one with the jostling crowds of laughing people of all ages. In fact, she'd never felt so happy and loose in her life. Twining an arm around his waist, she sighed happily. "You were right and I was wrong. I *loved it*."

"Well, good," he said, grinning down at her. "By the way, did I tell you how well the cap becomes you?"

Grinning back, she reached up and quacked the bill of Donald Duck, jammed over her sophisticated hairdo. "Yours must have been especially designed for you." She barely got the words out before going into a paroxysm of laughter over Goofy, perched on his head with ears hanging beside his cheeks. Fanning her face, she gasped out, "I don't know what's wrong with me. I feel as drunk as I did that first night, and I haven't had anything but lemonade."

"Laughter is intoxicating, pretty lady." Alec wrapped his arm tighter around her slender shoulders. He hadn't been lying that he was still kid enough to love Disneyland, but seeing a superior beauty like Bunny turn into a happy kid with him was the ultimate pleasure. He felt happier than he'd been in a long time, perhaps ever in his life. "I'm feeling a little drunk myself."

Snuggling her head against the curve where his arm

met his chest, she couldn't seem to stop smiling. "You made an idiot of yourself in there, you know it? Do you have a single inhibition to your name?"

He patted down his pockets. "Not when I last checked."

"I'll have to admit with your mustache, you're a natural at yo-ho-hoing with the Pirates of the Caribbean. Though it wasn't a smooth move to fall out of the boat."

All sorts of responses flashed through Alec's body when she giggled into his shirt. He lifted her cap and kissed the top of her head, then replaced it. "Well, you did your share, too, lady. You sang a talented falsetto in Small World. Didn't I tell you a few hours in this place is guaranteed to melt the steeliest hype?"

"You didn't mention that, but it's not the place, it's you. You're a horrible influence on me."

"It's my calling to corrupt the little old image right off you." Leaning forward, he kissed the back of her neck as she unlocked the car door.

The brush of his mustache sent a response tingling through Bunny's body. Stepping around to put the open door between them, she gazed at him with a sensual, teasing smile on her lips. "Are you getting ideas again, stranger?"

"Millions of them." Resting his forearms on top of the door, he loved the way her face had been softened by laughter and made human by the cap. People were flowing around them, cars starting, moving out, but Alec was so aware of Bunny, they might as well have been alone. "Surely we can't still be strangers after laughing and playing together?"

"I'm even a stranger to myself, after today's experience." Which reminded her of George and caused an ambivalent frown. "I called my father last night to say I'd drop in if I had time before catching the plane. If you come and meet him, you'll understand me better." Biting her lip, she quickly added, "I love him dearly and admire him for being a successful, aggressive man, but I'll be the first to admit he's quite daunting. Don't feel obligated to say yes."

"I'd consider it a privilege to meet your father," he said, surprised and gratified that she'd opened a door for him to step into her personal life.

"See, that's the problem. He may not think it's a privilege to meet you." Blowing out a breath, she snapped her finger at one of his Goofy ears. "Especially if you show up in this thing."

Alec pushed the cap up, letting brown hair fall over his forehead. "I take it you're afraid the great George may not be impressed with your little old Woodbox boyfriend. I've run into a lot of people with attitude problems after associating with the retarded for so many years. Trust me, I've got a tough skin and I can hold my own."

"Yes, I'm sure you probably can, but . . ." She climbed into the driver's seat, torn because she didn't know any longer which of two different worlds she belonged in, and wanted so badly to have Alec fit into her old life. After he'd gotten into the passenger seat, she glanced at him. "I'd feel terrible if George didn't appreciate you."

Her description of her father hadn't induced him to drop his mistrust of fathers in general. That, combined with her feeling uncomfortable over him not fitting in, turned him stubborn. Jamming Goofy down over his forehead, he folded his arms over his chest. "Don't expect me to pretend I'm someone other than who I am. I can't do that, not even for you."

"That's not what I meant! I like you exactly the way you are." Bunny started the car, thinking it was fortunate they had a plane to catch, leaving them with only limited time for the encounter.

The freeways were busy and it was nearly 8:00 P.M. when she drove into the Beverly Hills neighborhood, winding between wooded hills, then up the long tree-lined drive. Stopping in front of the house, she glanced at Alec. "This is your last chance to back out."

He shook his head, a goofy ear dangling by each cheek. "Nope, you've worked me up into a fever of curiosity."

If he was going to wear the damned cap, then she had no choice but to leave Donald on her head. Turning grimly toward the house, she walked up onto the front porch without looking at him again.

"I was afraid you weren't coming, pet," her father said, opening the door before she reached it. He looked very continental, wearing a knotted scarf in the neck of his white silk shirt. "What on earth is that thing on your head?" he said next, lifting a brow.

Giving a laugh, Bunny quacked her bill and babbled an explanation. "We went to Disneyland and the freeways were backed up, so it took longer than I expected. Now we've only got a few minutes, but I couldn't go back without seeing you."

"I'm glad you had time," he said, giving her a hug. "I worried that you might hold my tirade over Faline against me."

"No, you're all I have, George." She pressed her face into his shoulder for a moment, then drew away. "I brought someone with me."

Turning to hold out a hand to Alec, standing right behind her, Bunny gave a surprised, relieved laugh.

"This is me too," he reminded her, grinning. He'd taken the cap off and put his tie, vest, and jacket back on before following her onto the porch.

"I'll be eternally grateful," she whispered. Taking his hand, she brought him into the foyer. "George, I'd like you to meet Alec Golightly from Portland, Or-y-gun. Alec, my father."

George's eyes could be as frigidly blue as her own when he wasn't happy about something, and they were icy now as he held out his hand. "How do you do, Alec. How very unique to meet you."

"How do you do, sir." Alec smiled angelically as he shook hands. "I might say the same about you."

"Yes." George led the way into the living room.

"Have a seat, Alec," he said, leaning an elbow on the fireplace mantel. "Outside of the fact that you work at the Woodbox, Bunny has told me remarkably little about you."

Mustache twitching, Alec remained on his feet, too, using his height as a four-inch advantage over Bunny's father. "I can't think of any reason why she should have, sir. Since you're interested, I'm involved in the plight of the developmentally disabled and building a boat in my backyard. I think that about sums me up."

Sitting in a brocaded armchair, Bunny grinned, knowing George had expected to cow the younger man with his superior attitude. Pleased that her Golightly Man could hold his own, she was delighted to supply the rest. "Alec is our general manager, and today he proved himself brilliant by talking Eleganté into letting us buy the Woodbox."

Looking as if doom were closing in, George listened to her relate the details. "Yes, that's wonderful. If you've accomplished what you set out to do, then you'll be coming home soon, won't you?"

"No, I'll stay until after the down payment is paid and everything is safely finalized."

"I see."

"Besides," Alec tossed in, "I'm only beginning to teach Bunny how to relax and enjoy life. It's hard to believe she had never visited Disneyland."

George's eyes widened; he was obviously startled to be put on the defensive. "Disneyland hardly seemed vital when she had a superior intellect. I gave her every advantage necessary to develop her potential. Nothing was left out."

Alec unbuttoned his jacket and hooked his thumbs in the small pockets of his vest. "Except, perhaps, learning to relax and enjoy herself."

George lifted a brow. "Are you suggesting women shouldn't be prepared for positions of business power?"

Alec smiled. "On the contrary, I'm particularly partial to brilliant, successful career women."

"Sure you are," Bunny muttered, crossing her knees and shoving Donald down over her forehead. She doubted any man was and resented his joking about so sore a subject.

George narrowed his eyes at Alec. "Then you aren't opposed to Bunny accepting a position with Faline Productions, which will make her very successful indeed."

Alec narrowed his eyes back. "It doesn't make any difference what either you or I think Bunny should do. Her life is her own to decide."

A genuine, warm smile lit George's face. "Since Bunny saw fit to tell me so little about you, Alec, perhaps you can understand that I've had some anxious moments. I'm very happy to have had this opportunity to meet you. My daughter is very precious to me, and I want only the best for her."

Alec's grin tilted his mustache up at the ends. "Then that's one thing we see eye to eye on, sir."

Dropping her head on the chair back, Bunny went

limp with relief. The two men she cared most about seemed to be on the verge of accepting each other. Given time, they might even like each other. Though being home reminded her that a relationship with Alec was still very much a dream. Sighing, she rose to her feet. "If you two are finished discussing me, we'd better go catch a plane."

After the farewells Bunny drove back onto the freeway and merged by the skin of her fenders into a line of cars. Alec looked out the windows at the slow-moving traffic, moving at a spasmodic twenty miles per hour. "Am I on the fast track now?"

"Smart Alec!" she said dryly, then laughed softly. "Poor George isn't accustomed to people standing up to him—that's all that saved you. It's hard to believe, but he's always been patient and loving to me."

Alec jerked his tie loose and sat sideways in the seat to gaze at her. "But it doesn't sound like he let you have a childhood."

"He did the best he knew how." Bunny tightened her fingers on the wheel, driving through the perpetual neon glow of the sprawling city. "Poor guy, my mother died in a car accident and left him with a toddler. He didn't know what girls needed and zeroed in on my intelligence. I wanted to please him, but I felt like a freak in the gifted programs and going to UCLA as a mere kid." She squinted against the smoggy halos around the sodium vapor lights. "I didn't have many friends, and none of the boys wanted to date Bernice, the dreaded curve breaker."

Feeling a rush of tenderness and sympathy, Alec placed a comforting hand around the back of her neck. "But obviously something happened to change things."

Melted by his sympathy, Bunny smiled slightly. "When George realized how lonely I was, he put me in charm school to learn how to say the right things, give PR smiles, and function beautifully in any situation. I had plastic surgery on my nose and chin, had eyeliner tattooed on, and learned makeup and hairstyling." She grinned at him. "And to eat tofu and bean sprouts, exercise, and to adorn my body."

Alec studied her beautiful profile, lit by the glow of the dash. "Bernice went underground, and Bunny emerged. Are you sorry or glad it happened?"

"Looking good and knowing how to act is better. But not that the people I want to know tend to be awed. The ones who try to get close usually want something from me."

"I can imagine," he said thoughtfully. "But things are different at the Woodbox, aren't they?"

"Yes, everyone there is so nice." Frowning, she exited the freeway. "Being around real women makes me wish my mother had lived to show me the feminine side of life. I've missed out on so much. Making a home, being around babies."

Alec felt his heart leap in alarm. "I've never known a more total woman than you, as is," he said quickly. "I'm partial to—"

"Oh, please don't say it again!" Bunny groaned.

"You're partial to brilliant women saving the Woodbox. Didn't you tell me you're nothing but a great big kid? Well, as I recall, high-school boys are looking for T and A, not brains."

He gave a sheepish laugh. "I'll plead the fifth on that one. Anything I say could be taken wrong and used against me."

After turning in the rental car, Bunny stood beside Alec in line to check in. "While we're on the subject, I should explain that after my metamorphosis, I had a problem with guys wanting to notch their . . . uh . . . pistol by bedding a glamorous woman. Nan called you a butterfly early on, so I thought you were one of them and went on the defensive when you made a pass."

"Since we're being honest, I'll admit I've had a light love affair a time or two, but I never thought of it as notching my . . . uh . . . pistol," he said, jacket slung over his shoulder hooked on one finger, briefcase in the other hand. Then a teasing grin lit his face. "Besides, you're a fine one to talk when you spend too damn many hours carrying on a love affair with a computer."

She quacked her bill and grinned back. "Why shouldn't I love my computer? It's faithful, eager to do my every wish, and may even be a little smarter than me. Unlike most men I know."

"Mmmm," he commented, plotting ways to seduce her away from her lover and win more time for himself.

SEVEN

It was almost 2:00 A.M. when Bunny got to the cottage and dropped into bed. The alarm went off as usual at 4:30. She hopped up, fired with enthusiasm and amazed at what a day of success and relaxation had done for her.

Dashing through her morning routine, she felt proud and amazed to have kept the bedroom and bathroom sparkling clean without help. The rest of the cottage, however, was still festooned with cobwebs, the carpet gray with accumulated dirt, and the kitchen too filthy to use for eating. Luckily Alec hadn't been inside since the first day and didn't know how bad things were. She also felt very territorial and fully intended to tackle the cleaning herself. Just as soon as she found the time.

Wearing a hot-pink spandex biking suit that rivaled the sunrise behind Hood, she hopped on her bike and pedaled down the street. The air was as clear and heady as fine wine. Early birds were chirping, patches of fog drifting, pines spreading their scent. It was eerily peaceful with so few cars on the streets. She'd miss her early Portland mornings when she went home again. When . . . ? If . . . ?

At the Woodbox she took off her helmet and folded a stick of gum into her mouth. The undistinguished-looking buildings were deserted at 5:20 A.M. An internal imp questioned what she was doing at a luckless kit-furniture factory, when the thought of coordinating Faline's important feminist films lit sparklers in her mind. With that thought, she realized her post-Enterprise burnout had passed without her knowing.

Squinting through her glasses, Bunny picked out the graystone house and cottage on the bluff across the misty river. If she did refuse Faline's offer, it would only be because of Alec. Say, she pondered, just speculating, say she were to fall in love with him. Could she make a happy life with a Golightly Man?

Not that anything as permanent as marriage, or even a serious affair, had come up. If Alec had something like that in mind, surely he would be sharing his inner feelings, dreams, and past. Maybe he wasn't a true butterfly, but he had admitted to frivolous sexual encounters. Was that all he wanted from her? The thought squeezed her heart so painfully, it felt like a coronary attack.

The sensation goaded her into the main building. Changing into a black pants suit, she turned on her computer and began evaluating the Woodbox sales records.

Going on modem, she began researching appropriate potential markets. That done, she mapped out the most lucrative places to visit and worked out travel arrangements.

Alec came in at 7:30 and called her into his office for a clandestine good-morning hug. Putting her uncertainties aside, she arched against his tall, tempting, masculine body.

"How long have you been here?" he murmured, fluttering more kisses over her face.

"For a while," she said, adding, "Lazy bones."

He lifted his head to smile down at her. "Don't you ever sleep?"

"I didn't need any after we had so much fun yesterday," she answered, laying her cheek over the beat of his heart.

He nuzzled her cheek. "Only I wish we'd had days and weeks of it instead of a few hours."

It confirmed her suspicion to hear he was thinking in terms of days and weeks, not forever. Bunny pulled away to pace the office. "We can't even afford to give up hours with a buyout to accomplish."

Alec watched her, so sleek and vital in her black pants suit, with not so much as a tired smudge under her eyes. He adored her to be career-oriented, but he wished she looked a little frazzled by her self-imposed demanding schedule. It worried him that she did seem to thrive on the fast track. "An hour or two now and then won't send the deal down the tube. Let's go to Astoria this weekend and watch the Columbia River crash into the ocean."

"I'll bet that's something!" Ambivalently she looked out the window at the powerful river, then glanced back at Alec. "But I wonder if you realize how much money Eleganté will probably ask for the Woodbox buildings, stock, and land. And they won't cut the price when they'd meant to write a closure off their income taxes."

"Boy, you're a bundle of joy this morning." He walked across the office and stood beside her. "If that's reality, I prefer a little fantasy, thank you."

"I've never been big on fantasy."

"Why doesn't that surprise me?"

Bunny watched a bus pull up in front of Packaging. The special troop climbed out and milled aimlessly around, waiting for the supervisors to bring them in. Smiling, she put her hand on Alec's arm. "Look, Tess and Dwight are holding hands. That's a real fantasy." Her smile died. "Sometimes I wish my life were as simple as theirs."

He lifted her hand to his lips. "It could be. I'd safely bet those two aren't worried about whether they're strangers."

"I wouldn't worry about being strangers if hand-holding was all we intended to do," Bunny said, withdrawing her hand. "Anyhow, I can't go to Astoria, because I'm making arrangements to go to North Carolina to talk to a furniture man George did some promotion for once."

He felt a leap of anxiety. "Business on the weekend?"

"Yes, a social sort of business invitation. With a little strategic PR I can butter him into teaching me a lot about furniture, and how to build up sales and growth potential. Which we'll need to attract the lenders for the down payment. All of which takes hard work and long hours." Her inner dynamo thrumming, she lifted her brows. "What are your thoughts?"

Alec glowered at her. "Yippee."

Two weekends later it was a rare sunshiny Sunday for early June. Dwight was paddling in the pool, waiting for Tess. Jake was sitting on the edge with his feet in the water, watching nothing. Alec was stretched out in a lounge chair wearing a droopy-brimmed hat, sunglasses, and swimming shorts, grumpily wishing Bunny were there too. He'd pushed his campaign for more time and fun too hard, and now she was mad enough at him to be tearing the cottage to ribbons.

He was so preoccupied, he didn't realize anyone had come into the backyard until a kiss landed on his cheek and a dry voice said, "If you aren't too terribly busy doing whatever you're doing, I have an hour to spend before rushing off to catch a plane."

"Hey, Ma, what is this, parents' month or something?" He gave his mother a hug from his reclining position, glad to see her dressed casually in a black skirt and blouse, with turquoise jewelry.

"Don't call me Ma," Frances Golightly said mildly.

"The term is over, so I'm on my way to San Francisco to join a friend on a trip to Machu Picchu."

"Male friend?"

"There are some things a son doesn't need to know about his mother." She greeted the two special men in the pool and they responded with delight, having known her from the beginning. Then she stretched out on the lounge chair beside Alec. "How's the Woodbox crisis progressing?"

"For every agonizing step we take forward, we seem to fall two backward. Eleganté wants a hellish down payment. Even if every employee throws his soul in the pot, we'll have to find other financial sources." Getting up, he rapped on the white-painted belly of the boat that had eaten most of his available funds. "If I had this baby finished, I could be traveling, too, instead of going crazy over the suspense."

Frances smiled sympathetically. "You would have had it done ages ago if as much activity were going on here in your backyard as there is at the cottage. When I drove up, I noticed rugs strewn on the porch and dust virtually fuming from the windows. Do you have guests arriving?"

Alec plopped back down on the lounge chair. "Not a guest. Bunny's living in it for a few months."

She gazed at him narrowly, a breeze stirring her silver hair. "*My* son has taken up with a woman named *Bunny*?"

In his phone calls, Alec had felt a mother didn't

need to know too much about her son's fatal attractions either, so he'd referred only vaguely to a nameless visiting expert. "I haven't taken up with her," he muttered, flinging one bare leg across the other. "Unfortunately."

"Oh?" A beat or two of curiosity passed. "If the cottage is an example, she seems quite energetic."

"She's that all right!" he said, folding his arms over his bare chest. "She's working off a mad over my insisting she take the damn weekend off."

Frances folded her arms, too, scowling. "*My* son saw fit to insist a woman stay home and clean house?"

"I did not insist she clean the house! She hasn't taken a day off since she came. She buries herself in her computer twelve hours a day, and uses the other twelve running around the country trying to raise the down payment. I am the boss, so I couldn't let her burn herself out, could I?" Bunny hadn't come anywhere near burning herself out, but he couldn't tell his mother that he wanted her to himself. Grudgingly he admitted, "I may have been a little, quote and unquote, overbearing about it."

"Let me get this straight. Are you saying this *Bunny* is the business expert you mentioned?"

"Well, yeah, I guess." He wished to hell he hadn't gotten into this conversation, knowing his mother had definite ideas on how he should be running his personal life. "I'm grateful for her help, but she goes at everything like a house afire. Take the damn cottage.

I'll bet she's down there ripping it apart stone by stone, plotting a more efficient house plan, instead of relaxing and recouping. I blame her father for her acting like that."

She threw him a jaundiced glance. "Now we're blaming parents for all the ills of the world, are we?"

"You might think so, too, if you met him. George mapped her life out for her the day she was born, and rather pointedly didn't think I fit in the plan." This had bothered Alec far more than he would ever have admitted to Bunny. "His only saving grace is that he seems to genuinely love her."

A bird trilled in a cedar tree as Frances gazed at Jake for a moment, then back at Alec. "I expect it's hard for you to accept and understand a warm paternal relationship, after your own father acted the way he did." She shifted angrily in the chair. "On second thought, maybe parents *are* the cause of the world's ills after all."

He reached over and patted his mother on the shoulder. "I grew up just fine, thanks to you. Now, let's leave the topic of my father in the grave where it belongs."

"Are you certain it's dead enough to be buried? Sometimes I wonder if you've ever come to terms with what happened. Perhaps it'd do you good to explore it."

"Mom, I'm fine," he said, his jaw tightening.

Frances reluctantly gave in and redirected the subject. "Am I justified in assuming you've developed a . . . uh . . . *friendship* with Bunny?"

"No, you aren't," Alec said irritably, wondering why she couldn't find something neutral to discuss. "She doesn't alight long enough to enjoy eating or drinking, much less to let me pin her down for a . . . uh . . . friendship."

His mother smiled inscrutably and got out of the lounge chair. "Then if there's nothing personal involved, I'm sure you won't object to my going over to the cottage. I'm dying of curiosity over this powerhouse."

Alec reared up and watched her walk toward the French doors. He went cold over the idea of the two strong-willed women he cared most about coming together. Especially when one of them was mad enough to spit. He couldn't think of any way to forestall it, so he jumped up and hurried after her. "I'd better go with you for your protection, Mom. She might stampede over you with a vacuum cleaner."

Bunny couldn't help laughing over the thought of herself, dirty, sweaty, her hair shapeless, no makeup, crouching on her elbows and knees, watching the wax dry on the kitchen linoleum. Her pink lace top and white satin hot pants were highly inappropriate, but the only expendable clothing she'd found in her closet.

Despite that, she felt very proud of having cleaned the entire cottage, almost all by herself. "I would have been lost without you, sweetie," she said to Tess, who was crouched beside her. Her hired helper had worked at a snail's pace, her major contribution being a knowledge of cleaning basics. Bunny would have wallowed in squalor before asking that pushy Alec how to do the silly chores.

Annoyingly, as if she'd conjured him up with a passing thought, he appeared in the kitchen doorway, with his shoulders, chest, and legs looking disgustingly spectacular in a swimsuit. An older woman was by his side.

"What in hell are you doing?" he asked, lifting his sunglasses to peer down at Bunny.

The visit excited Tess far more than it did Bunny. "We watching the wax," she sang out. "Bunny Lady didn't think it be shiny dry, like wet." Beaming, she jumped up and threw her arms around the woman. "I glad to see you, Golightly Mom!"

Summoning what dignity she could, Bunny climbed up onto her feet. "Sweetie, why don't you get in your swimsuit and join Dwight in the pool?" When Tess had complied, she turned icy eyes on Alec. "I don't believe I heard you knock."

"I guess I forgot," he said, rasping his knuckles over the hair on his bare chest. "I came over to introduce my mother, Frances Golightly. Mom, this is Bernice Fletcher. Better known as Bunny."

"Your *mother*, how wonderful!" Jerking her hot pants down over the half-moons in back, Bunny barely suppressed an urge to decapitate him with a kitchen knife.

Radiating a PR smile, she extended a grubby hand to Frances. "I'm delighted to meet you, Ms. Golightly. Alec told me you helped decorate his house. Then he had the gall to describe the lovely pieces you furnished it with as 'contemporary or something.' "

Frances shook Bunny's hand, her eyes bright with curiosity. "I'm very pleased to meet you, too, and also rather astonished. That son of mine has apparently been tight-lipped as a rubber band, because somehow I expected a more burned-out ash from what he said." Her gaze flicked over Bunny's face, see-through lace top, and labor-smudged legs. "So you're an efficiency expert."

Cringing inside, Bunny flicked a glance and a dangerous smile at Alec, then turned to his mother. "When that son of yours met me, he fell into the trap of thinking a woman needed to wear her brain in full view to be able to do a good job. I sincerely hope you won't make that mistake, Ms. Golightly."

"Never, my dear, and please call me Frances," she said with a delighted smile. "I wonder if that son of mine told you what I do as a life work?"

"That son of yours hasn't told me one single thing about his family." Bunny flicked another glance at him. "We're essentially strangers yet."

Alec mashed the droopy brim of his hat down over his forehead and leaned a shoulder against the door frame. "Don't bother including that son of hers in the conversation. But since you're wondering, Ma happens to be a—"

"Shhh, let me guess."

"And don't call me Ma!"

Bunny deemed the woman to be in her fifties, face etched with hardships, kindness, and humor. With a stocky body dressed rather dowdily in a skirt and blouse, Native American jewelry, and earthy sandals, she looked like your basic housewife. Still, she wasn't wearing a wedding ring and Bunny wasn't about to fall into any traps either. "Something creative. Crafts, pottery?"

Frances laughed slyly. "I have been known to do both crafts and pottery when I'm not busy teaching graduate-level anthropology at the University of Washington. That's why I'm not likely to jump to conclusions about other women."

Bunny stared. "Good grief, really! I'm incredibly impressed."

Alec grinned. "Ma has as good a brain and just as much spunk as you, Princess. That's why I'm so partial to brilliant, successful women. Maybe you should rethink some of your preconceptions."

Stepping closer, Bunny poked a finger with a chipped nail at the bulging biceps in his folded arm, not quite ready to forgive him yet. "My preconceptions do not depend on your mother's brain, they depend on your attitude."

Watching with amused interest, Frances said, "I understand Alec left you to clean his filthy cottage."

"I did not leave her with the job, Ma," he said, his green eyes flaring.

"Don't call me Ma."

"Mommy, dearest," he murmured through clenched teeth, and put an arm a teensy bit too tightly around Bunny's shoulders. "I offered to have someone clean for her. I even offered to do it myself."

Laying her hand against his chest, Bunny closed the fingers a teensy bit threateningly on curly hair. "He did offer, Frances, that's the truth. I had to kick him out because he was a touch overly autocratic in his offers. And called me stubborn as a mule."

Alec lifted her hand and replaced it on his hairless shoulder. "Our contract specifies that I'm the boss, so as long as you're working at the Woodbox, your well-being is my responsibility, Princess. And I doubt you would have blown up about it if you hadn't needed the time off. I wanted you to *rest*, not to work." In actuality, he wanted her career-oriented, not domestic.

Bunny maintained her sweet smile, a steely glint in her eyes. "You may have been right about my needing time off, and you may be the boss, but you overstepped your authority when you implied I couldn't handle housework." She glanced around the sparkling-clean kitchen. "If your mother weren't here, I'd take you on a tour and show you how wrong you were."

His mother had been watching the exchange with knowing, speculative interest. "Unless you were planning a private tour, I'd love to see this miracle too."

Bunny pulled away from Alec's arm, a proud smile lighting her face. "Well, I'd love to show you. It sounds silly, but I really enjoyed polishing up this little house."

Feeling out of sorts and left out, Alec followed the two women through the house, listening to them discuss decorating like a couple of hausfraus. He didn't mind so much that Bunny had washed the walls and vacuumed the carpets and furniture several shades lighter, but he began wishing he'd left her at the computer when he realized she'd gone cutesy. There were frilly curtains in the kitchen, and a violet-sprigged shower curtain and lavender towels with lace borders hanging in the bathroom. Ruffled throw pillows were heaped on his patchwork comforter in the bedroom.

Ending her tour in the living room, Bunny turned to him and said, "Seeing must be believing. Are you ready to eat crow now, Golightly Man?"

Plopping down on the sofa, Alec said grumpily, "If my mother weren't here, I'd drop on my knees and eat my crows in humble pie."

"Don't let me stop you," Frances murmured, sitting in an armchair.

Smothering a laugh, Bunny sat a discreet distance from him on the sofa. "All right, I'll let you off the hook. You were right, I wouldn't have known where to begin without Tess's help. She even had to show me how to turn on the vacuum cleaner."

That sounded a little more optimistic, so he bent sideways to give her a peck on the cheek. "Hey, Ma, have you ever heard of a woman reaching so ripe an age without ever having cleaned a house?"

"Wait a minute, I'm not *that* ripe," Bunny said, diplomatically twitching her hot pants down and moving farther away from him. "And don't call your mother Ma."

Frances gave a delighted laugh. "I do believe I've found a sympathetic, kindred spirit." She paused, glancing from one to the other. "Did I understand correctly that you and Alec are business partners?"

"I'm not a partner, just a temporary consultant."

"Son, wouldn't it be a good idea to talk her into staying permanently? The . . . uh . . . Woodbox needs new, energetic blood."

"Ma, you're as transparent as glass." He got up and looked out the window, fingertips tucked in the band of his swimming shorts. "Naturally the . . . uh . . . Woodbox would love her to stay permanently. God knows, I've tried to talk her into it."

"Yes, he has, but . . ." Bunny glanced ambivalently at his sensual body, then hitched herself forward on the sofa. "If I made so big a step as working at the Woodbox, I'd have to be absolutely certain it was the right thing for me. Because if I go home, I have a chance to be an associate producer for Faline Productions."

"My heavens, *Faline*!" Frances exclaimed. "How I wish I'd seen her consciousness-raising movies back when I was a meek little housewife, waiting on my lord and master. Things might have gone differently in our family."

Bunny studied her curiously. "I can't picture you catering to a lord and master."

"In a previous incarnation." Frances waved it off.

"But working with Faline is a once-in-a-lifetime opportunity."

Alec looked back from the window, lifting his mustache in a warped smile. "Some decision, huh? Why would she settle for money, challenge, glamour, and prestige when she could have—" He bit off the *me* and substituted, "The Woodbox."

Frances gave him a piercing look. "That philosophy applies to you, too, son—the other way around."

Getting up, she walked toward the door. "Now that I've meddled beyond forgiveness in your private lives, I'll go catch the plane. My friend and Machu Picchu are waiting."

After hugging Alec, she put her arms around Bunny. "My dear, you've made me realize how nice it might be to have a daughter again. Oh, well."

Standing in the yard after watching Frances drive out of sight, Alec brushed a smear of housecleaning grime off Bunny's cheek. "If you're done with this damn cottage, can we go swimming and have some fun for the last measly hours of the weekend?"

"Sounds heavenly. I'll get my suit on and meet you at the pool."

EIGHT

When Bunny came through the French doors and walked across the patio, Alec melted with longing. Her white suit left her back completely bare, her hips revealed to the iliac crest on each side, and her front fully covered with a sling around the neck. It was modest by modern standards, but she was so lusciously lithe, she would have looked sexy in a gunnysack. "How do you always manage to look fabulous?"

"With biking, tofu, and bean sprouts." She glanced at him up and down, her sunny blue gaze lingering on the pelt of brown hair on his chest. "I couldn't say it with your mother around, but you look pretty good yourself, Golightly Man."

He patted his flat stomach and grinned. "Pizza, burgers, and fries."

"You and your junk-food fetish! It's not fair that you can eat anything you want and don't look like a blimp." Sidestepping his teasing reach, she walked over to the pool.

Dwight and Tess were treading water at the other end, caught up in gazing at each other but feeling no obvious need to talk or play. Jake was sitting on the edge. "What are you doing, sweetie?" Bunny asked.

"Watching." The vacantly handsome young man nodded at a bug bobbing on the lapping waves.

"How interesting," she murmured. Wondering why all three weren't bored spitless, Bunny dived in and swam furious laps for a time. Then she climbed out and began toweling her hair fluffy.

Moving over to the edge of the pool, Alec let his gaze flow with the rivulets of water running down over her high breasts, tiny waist, curved hips, and shapely legs. He smiled up at her. "We both know the other's parent now—are we still strangers?"

"Yes, I find you very strange." She snapped her towel at him. "Especially after you pulled a trick like popping a mystery mother on me. Me on the floor in hot pants, with my butt in the air."

"Oh, it was a sight to behold, all right," he said, his mustache twitching. "But it didn't dampen my mother's enthusiasm one bit. I hope her innuendos didn't offend you. She shares your opinion that I'm wasting my potential on the Woodbox, and thinks marriage might inspire me to bigger and better things."

"Would it?" Bunny asked, sitting beside him with her feet dangling in the water.

"We may never know." He glanced wistfully at her. "It'd take a unique woman to consider marriage with me."

Since that sounded more like warning her off than an opening, she turned her eyes toward the black bug bobbing on the lapping waves. It actually was quite relaxing, even rather fascinating, to wonder how long it would take to bob across the pool. Thoughts bobbed on the gentle waves of her mind. "Meeting Frances made me realize how much I missed not having a mother in my life."

"Yeah, Mom is neat, but I missed out by not having a father too." Alec rested his elbows on his knees and frowned at the evergreen trees beyond the pool.

Moving her foot to see if increased wave action would hasten the bug's progress, she went back to her own musings. "If I'd had a mother like Frances, maybe I wouldn't be driving myself mad, trying to decide what to do with my life. I'd probably be making a home and doing woman things."

The conversation had taken a turn he didn't like, but he couldn't stop himself from testing how hopeless the situation was. "And being a mother yourself, I suppose?"

"I couldn't say about that. If I didn't have a mother, how would I know how to be one? Which seems a terrible cheat." She glanced up at him. "Have you ever thought about being a father?"

Bending over, he splashed the damn bug out of the water. He wanted to open up and tell her everything, but he couldn't get the words past the barrier in his throat. "The special people in my troop are my kids. That's about all the fathering I can handle."

"Yes, I see how it could be." Gazing at Dwight and Tess, bobbing on the waves, and gentle Jake on the edge of the pool, Bunny felt a sense of protectiveness. She wondered if that was the same as feeling maternal. A thought popped up. "What happened to your father? Did he die?"

"Later, when I was grown up," he said shortly.

Another thought occurred to her. "What did your mother mean, that it might be fun to have a daughter *again*? Do you have a sister?"

Frustrated with his inability to answer her simple, legitimate questions, Alec said, "What in hell is this preoccupation with my sordid past?" Throwing off his hat and dark glasses, he launched himself into the pool.

Stunned by his reaction, Bunny watched him thrash away. She was on the brink of falling in love with a man who either didn't trust or didn't care enough to share his feelings. The quandary went around and around in her mind. What did she want? An affair? Marriage? A month? Feeling the way she did, could she bear to leave him and go with Faline?

Jumping up, she ran back to the cottage to pack for the next day's marketing trip to Cleveland. She needed the three days away to analyze her feelings.

Cursing under his breath, Alec glared at the jammed nut stopping him from bolting a bunk to the inside of his boat. Nothing was going right. Bunny had been gone two days, another to go, and he was lonelier than he'd ever been in his life. So lonely, he'd come home from work, changed into old jeans and a ragged T-shirt, and sunk into the bowels of his boat for solace.

He couldn't delude himself any longer; he'd fallen in love with his untouchable goddess. Then he'd gone right ahead and put his dream-come-true in jeopardy. Only the worst kind of bastard would tease for closeness, then shut her out when she asked a question about his past. Liberally despising himself, he realized he'd acted like one of her damn pistol notchers.

Well, it'd never happen again, he vowed, forcing the wrench against the damned stuck nut. If she'd give him another chance, he'd prove himself before sniffing around. No matter how desirable she was, or how eagerly his body begged.

"Are you down there?" came an angel's husky voice from above. "I've been looking all over for you."

Alec jumped. The wrench slipped, but he didn't feel the gouge when his knuckle contacted the nut. Flooded by more important feelings, he looked up at a head haloed by gold, framed by the main hatch. Going limp with an explosion of relief, joy, hope, and more, he flopped onto his back. "You're home."

"Brilliant deduction, genius." The head withdrew and two sandaled feet stepped down the companionway ladder, followed by two lovely slender legs, a pair of temptingly svelte hips in white shorts, a tiny waist, and two perky breasts under a flowered tee, then Bunny's marvelous smiling face. No glasses. No gum.

"Your car was here, so I knew you must be too," she sang out, sounding full of zip and vinegar. For some reason she had pink silver-dollar-sized spots on her cheekbones for the first time in a long time. "I searched the house, but almost didn't look here in the boat." Stopping beside him, she grinned. "I didn't realize you worked on this thing, I thought you just talked about it."

"Once in a while, when things get really tough," Alec said, resisting temptation like a trooper as he gazed up from his prone position at the delectable view above him. "I didn't expect you until tomorrow."

"I finished my business early," she said, hunkering down to sit on one heel beside him. "And I figured out what I want out of life too."

"Out of life . . . ?" With the delectable sight now in direct line with his eyes, life in general wasn't at the forefront of his mind. Sitting up, he tried to firm his resolutions by scrubbing both hands over his face. "What'd you figure out?"

"Oh, your hand is bleeding!" Bunny exclaimed, going down on both knees beside him. "How'd you do that?"

"I haven't the vaguest idea." He stared at his hand as if it belonged to someone else, then wiped the blood off his knuckle with the tail of his T-shirt. "It's nothing, just a scratch."

"It isn't nothing, it's you, and you're everything," she said softly. "That's what I figured out."

He lifted his eyes to her face. "Huh?"

Her lips curved in a smile. "I want to make your *ouchies* all better . . . among other things." Taking his big hand in her two soft, delicate ones, she closed her lips around his knuckle, tending the slight scratch with widening circles of her tongue.

The warm, moist touch ran like fire through Alec's body. "I'm still not exactly certain what you're talking about, Princess," he said, his voice going husky.

"I'm talking about overcomplicating things and talking myself out of everything I ever wanted in life up until now. I don't intend to do it any longer, Golightly Man." Turning his hand over, she worked her tongue in circles over his inner wrist.

"Oh, God, don't do that unless you want—"

Wondering what in hell had happened to the ice maiden, Alec came up on his knees and wrapped his arms around her. "I don't know what in the devil is going on, but I sure do like it."

Arching against him, Bunny curled her arms around his neck and gazed laughingly into his face. "I had lots of time to contemplate what might happen if I quit analyzing how I feel and how you feel, and what might happen if I do this or you do that. I thought about how you taught me to have fun at Disneyland, and wondered if lovemaking could be like going to an amusement park too."

"More like shopping in a toy store, actually." His mustache tilted up in a sultry smile; his eyes turned into a tropical sea. "You thought all that, did you?"

"And more. Like how all anyone has are the moments. This one point in time. I want to spend my moments with you, learning how to play."

His grin broadened. "Are you asking for a guided tour through the toy store?"

Unclasping a hand, Bunny touched a fingertip to his full lower lip. "Now you've got the picture! And you're the resident expert at grand tours."

"You betcha," Alec whispered, crushing her against him. "I missed you so much, Princess. You acted so cold and silent before you left. I thought you were mad at me."

"I wasn't angry, just confused about what I wanted. I missed you, too, just as much, maybe more." Pressing her face into his shoulder, she breathed in the citrusy, very masculine scent of a working man. "I dreamed about feeling your body against mine all the while I was gone. The days we have together are a gift and shouldn't be wasted."

"Being here with you at this moment in time is the most precious gift I've ever received." Tilting her chin up with his fingers, Alec looked down into her lovely face. "But what about being strangers? I acted like a hound when I didn't answer your question about my sister and the past. I've kicked myself ever since."

"I realized in Cleveland that I know all I need to know

about you already. You're a sweet, caring man." Smiling, she traced the shape of the muscles under his shirt with her fingertips. "And since you took the Woodbox over, my knees absolutely melt every time you act forceful and dynamic. On top of that, you're incredibly sexy."

Alec felt his face go hot with pleasure and passion. "If you keep talking like that, Princess, I'll have to take over this seduction and show you all the dynamic you can handle. As a matter of fact, I have a bottle of champagne chilling in the refridge, clean sheets on my bed, and all the niceties ready and waiting to do this special occasion up right. I might even find a rose or two in the garden. Let's go up to the house."

Bunny glanced around the cozy, private little boat cabin, at the satiny wood floor, cleanly painted cream walls. Faint evening light was filtering through the rectangular windows. The bunk was only half-attached, but its mattress was lying on the floor in invitation. "This is the perfect place for us to make love the first time. On your boat of dreams. Teach me to sail free, Golightly Man."

It seemed to Alec his heart was swelling large enough to burst out of his chest. "This is the best and only dream I have," he whispered, gazing into her molten-blue eyes and at the spots of passion on her cheeks. "You and me, the first man and woman in all eternity to make love."

Lowering his head, he covered her mouth with his. Then he drove himself wild with sensation by running his tongue ever so slowly over the inner surfaces of her lips, exploring deeper into a warm, sweet heaven.

On their knees, facing each other, he gentled his hands up under her tee, measured her small waist, grazed over her ribs, and cupped her braless breasts, rubbing the nipples with his thumbs. "You were right when you said Disneyland is rinky-dinky kid stuff," he whispered against her mouth. "This is the real thing."

"Oh, yes . . . oh—" Bunny's heart leaped into a bounding race, her breath into irregular gasps. An arrow seemed to shoot from her nipples to the core of her body. "I didn't realize a simple touch could feel so indescribable. There must be some kind of magic between us."

"The magic doesn't begin until we explore toyland." Pinching each erect nipple lightly with his fingers, he grinned down at her and pressed his thigh between her legs, moving against her sensitive, throbbing parts. "Do you like that, sweetheart?"

"Yes . . . *yes*, I do!" Clutching his shoulders, she threw back her head in a moan of need. "Alec, please . . ."

"Yes, Princess, I want you too . . . so much. I want to look at you."

Drawing back, he pulled her tee up over her head. The sensation of his fingers unbuttoning, unzipping, easing her shorts and panties down over her hips, exploring clefts and mounds, secret places, was almost too much to bear.

Pulling her to her feet, he slipped off her shorts, panties, and sandals. His eyes flickered with green fire, caressing every sleek curve and line of her body. "You are so incredibly beautiful, Bunny, sweetheart. A truly spectacular woman."

Her body was aflame with the touch of his gaze, a fire that burned away her old fears about being loved for her image. It just didn't matter. "If I'm beautiful, it's for you," she said softly. "I want to see you and touch you too." A teasing smile curved her lips. "I haven't had a chance to shop for treasures yet."

A grin lighting his face, Alec held out his arms. "Here I am for the browsing, Princess. Need a shopping cart?"

Bunny laughed softly. "If I see anything I want, I'll take it in my hands."

Heart racing with excitement, she pulled his shirt over his head, loving the curly brown hair covering his chest. His breathing turned ragged when she kissed his nipples, then kissed the line of hair down over his stomach. Laughing softly, she ran her hands over his belt buckle to cup the turbulence behind his fly. "What have we here?"

"It's a mystery to me," Alec said with a gasp, running his fingers into her cloud of hair. "It wasn't there before you turned up."

Trembling with eagerness, cheeks flaming, she unbuckled and unzipped, then pushed his jeans and briefs down over his long legs until he kicked them off with his feet. Gazing at the power of his sex, she whispered, "Why, you selfish thing, you've been keeping your most fascinating toys to yourself."

"What do you mean? I've been trying to share them

with you ever since we met." Laughing, flushed with desire, Alec grabbed her arms and lowered her onto the mattress. "And I'm just tickled pink to hand them over now."

"Do they come with instructions?"

"I'll give you instructions!"

She gave a shriek of laughter as he brushed her from neck to furry V with his mustache. Then she almost cried out with the sensation of his sucking first one nipple and then the other. His mustache brushing against her breasts was an exquisite torture.

Laughter dying, he sat back on his feet beside her, his hands on his thighs, and slowly ran his gaze over her, from toes to the top of her tousled amber mane. "Under all the glamour is a sweet, gentle, unique woman, the real Bunny who got lost somewhere along the way. That's the woman I'm making love to."

Tears welling in her eyes, she felt all her doubts evaporate. Laying both hands on his chest, she felt his heart beating strongly for her. "Oh, my darling, I can't think of words grand enough to describe how wonderful you are to tell me that."

"To have you call me darling is as wonderful as it gets," he whispered in a husky voice. "That we're here like this, and you're giving me joy is a miracle."

"Darling, darling, darling." Curling her fingers around his upper arms, she pulled him toward her. "I want to give you all the joy and happiness in the world."

Hungrily she tormented his body with fingers and tongue. In a fever pitch of desire, he grabbed her hands and held her captive while he teased her into a rage of pleasure with the talent of a sorcerer. He plundered her body with his tongue until she cried out, "Alec . . . I can't wait. Take me now!"

Braced on his elbows, he looked down into her face as he lowered himself and entered with a thrust, filling her. "You're mine now. We're one, Princess."

"Oh, my darling . . ." She couldn't speak around the joy of being filled with him, of moving with him in a demanding rhythm. Panting and whimpering against his neck, she exploded in a towering climax.

Even before the spasms faded, he arched his head back and gave a cry, shuddering with his release. Whispering words of love, he sank back down and pressed his face into the curve of her neck.

Drifting mindlessly, Bunny floated down like a spent leaf falling from a tree. Breath racing in short gasps, she held his big body tightly against her, feeling the miracle of his heart racing against her chest. There was no world other than this tiny one inside the boat, peopled only by herself and this infinitely thrilling, marvelous man.

Moments later, an eternity, Alec lifted his head, his eyes filled with a sea of feeling, a tremulous smile on his lips. Touching her face with his lips, he traced each feature as if imprinting something precious in his memory. "I think I've just visited paradise."

"Paradise . . ."

As she gazed into his sweet, rugged face she realized the inner emptiness she'd felt for so long was gone. "How odd," she whispered, "I've just given myself without expecting anything, and I feel complete for the first time in my life."

NINE

Paradise, magic, toyland, heaven. Alec had visited them all in making love to Bunny. Now he ached for it to last forever. The impossible dream. The biggest fantasy of them all. Still one with her body, he dipped his head and nibbled her lips, kissed her cheekbones, her eyelids, the tip of her nose. Then he made a cautious venture. "I think I'm almost falling in love with you."

"I think you're making an infamous almost declaration in the heat of passion, Golightly Man." Tracing the arch of his forceful brow with a finger, down his ravaged nose, she finally touched his mouth and smiled tremulously. "In the heat of passion, I might say I'm almost falling in love with you too. How about that for infamous?"

He wasn't sure if she was venturing as cautiously toward revealing her feelings as he was or teasing. At least she hadn't thrown his tentative declaration back in his face. "Which makes it a day of infamy to live forever in my memory, so I'd better not squash you." Lifting himself away, he lay on his side, an arm cocked under his head, gazing at her. "Seems we've come to an interesting *almost* point in our relationship."

Bunny turned on her side, facing him, head supported on one hand, the other drifting over the shape of his shoulder and chest. "Darling," she whispered, testing the feel of it. "Darling. I'll have to admit this has been a unique business relationship."

Grinning, he touched a finger to each raspberry of a nipple tilted perkily at him. "Funny business in a toy store."

An answering grin lit her face and her hand slipped lower on his body. "I'll just bet you played with toy pistols when you were a boy, didn't you?"

"*Make my day*. Sure, I played cops and robbers with the best of them, but I swear I have never notched a pistol in my life. What'd you play when you were a kid?"

Bunny snorted a laugh. "It shouldn't surprise you to hear my favorite toy was a calculator. You know how most people get old and go into a second childhood? Well, you're guiding me into my first. Three months ago I would have been appalled if someone had suggested I'd act like I did when I came on your boat tonight."

"Yeah, speak of a bad influence." Alec curved a big hand over the indentation of her waist. "Here I was, minding my own business, bolting in a bunk—"

"Screwin' around," she murmured, sniggering.

He rolled his eyes. "*Bolting* in a bunk, when you came along with your bag of Christmas toys and other gifts. What got into you?"

Frowning thoughtfully, she watched her fingers play through the damp curls of hair on his chest. "I lost a lot of sleep in Cleveland, thinking about how attracted we were to each other and about our goals being different, and that we might not be together very long. Everything seemed so hopeless."

"Yeah," Alec agreed unhappily. "Did you come up with a solution, I hope?"

"No, unfortunately. Which started me thinking about Dwight and Tess, and how they reach out and enjoy each other, just looking and holding hands. I'm sure they don't question where their relationship might go; they just take comfort and pleasure in it. They made me realize I'm cheating myself by overanalyzing everything. I decided to grab the moment and let the tomorrows take care of themselves." Smiling, she spread her fingers on his chest. "The genius is learning from your special troop."

"Oh, they have a wealth of logic the rest of us miss in our race for knowledge."

Alec watched his hand rising and falling with her breathing, awed that she'd come to a point of trusting and giving openly, without needing to know his past. In the face of her acceptance he didn't want to be a stranger any longer.

Glancing in something akin to panic at her beautiful, loving face, he swallowed dryly, his Adam's apple convulsing. "Speaking of my troop, I shouldn't have brushed you off when you asked about my sister."

Bunny curved her hand over the base of his neck. "I don't need to know if it's hard for you to talk about your past, darling."

"But I need to tell you."

"Then I'll listen."

Turning on his back, Alec lay silently for a time, but the words still wouldn't move around the throat barrier. He sat up with a wry smile. "Sounds stupid, but I can't talk about it without my clothes on."

"I don't see that as a bit stupid." Bunny laughed softly. "I'm a great one for dressing for the occasion, remember?"

"Right, there's something to be said for it."

Standing up, he pulled on his briefs and jeans and slipped his faded T-shirt over his head. Barefoot, he crouched beside the bunk and picked up his wrench.

Erasing all emotion from his mind allowed him to speak around the barrier. "My sister was born when I was five. By the time she was three, no one could pretend she wasn't severely retarded. Testing proved it was a congenital glitch picked up from my father's chromosomes." He glanced at her. "Jake is genetic, too, and reminds me of her."

"Oh, Alec, how sad." Slipping into her shorts and tee, Bunny sat on the wood floor beside him.

Muscles bulging, he forced the wrench against the

jammed nut, grunting as he went into the hard part of the story. "My father was an up-and-coming Harvard lawyer, and he couldn't cope with facing the day-to-day evidence that he was genetically 'flawed.' So when I was nine, he left. I never saw him again."

"You mean he turned his back on you too?" She put her hand on his bent thigh. "But that was cruel! It must have hurt terribly."

Alec concentrated on forcing the nut off the bolt. "Oh, yes, it hurt, because up until then I'd been Daddy's little boy. I assume he wanted to pretend none of it had happened. Being a lawyer, he finagled things until all my mother got was minimum child support, not nearly enough, since Carol had other congenital problems that required medical treatment." He gave a fierce, angry yank. The nut came loose and the wrench flew. "Dammit!"

Never looking up, he restarted the nut and tightened it before going on. "Despite the odds, my mother managed to recertify a teaching degree, stave off starvation, and still give us loving care. I tended Carol and played big brother, beating up the bullies who chanted 'dummy, dummy.'" He glanced at Bunny and touched his flattened nose and gouged chin. "I didn't always win the battles."

Moving to the other end of the bunk, he inserted a bolt, screwing on the nut. Following, she knelt beside him, her hand on his shoulder. "You never had a childhood either, did you?"

"At least I went to Disneyland." He glanced up with a wry smile, then looked down to apply the wrench. "When I started working at the Woodbox, there was more money and things were easier. Carol died when I was seventeen."

Bunny moved her arm around his neck and rested her face against his shoulder. "You loved her very much, didn't you?"

He nodded. "When she died, a little star blinked out in my world."

"So you lit some back up again with the troop."

"Yeah, that's about the size of it." Alec slipped the teak bunk board in place. "My old man died of a heart attack five years ago and left me his worldly goods, including the house and the vintage Mustang."

She studied his rugged profile. "Didn't it seem almost like a slap in the face at that point?"

"But the legacy gave me financial freedom, so I could concentrate on a troop of retarded people, which is a slap back, considering."

Alec tossed the wrench up in a spin and deftly caught it, trying to force himself to tell the rest. That testing had proven he'd inherited his father's genetic makeup. A vasectomy had relieved him of the fear that he might pass the flaw on to children of his own. But it had also left him feeling half a man, certain his only chance at happiness was with a dynamic career woman like Bunny, who didn't care about babies and being a mother.

Gazing into her lovely, brilliant face, he wasn't sure

enough of her to reveal his deficiencies. "So . . . that's it, I guess."

"I'm glad you told me, darling," she said, smiling tenderly. "You have the kind of background where a child could grow up warped, but you grew up kind and sweet enough to take on your special troop."

"I'm not sweet, I just like beating up on bullies. That's my calling in life, along with corrupting you." He tapped the wrench gently on the inwardly slanting wall of the cabin. "And building a dream boat. Want a guided tour?"

Bunny nodded, sensing he needed to back away from the heart-wrenching story he'd told so emotionlessly. "I'd love one."

Alec put the wrench down and rose to his bare feet. It was night outside now, and a bulb on an extension cord over his work area was the only lighting, playing up the cream-painted walls. "Terminology-wise, the windows are called port lights, the floor is the cabin sole, the stairs are a companionway ladder, and the door is a hatch."

"I'll file all that in my data banks," she murmured, grinning.

"I certainly hope so, Miz Fletcher." Carrying the light, Alec pointed out areas. "There's where I'll put a built-in table and seating, and the galley next to it. The engine is behind that bulkhead, and behind the other is the head—a john, to the uninitiated."

Eyes sparkling, Bunny lifted her aristocratic nose. "I never go in johns or heads."

"Then you'll have to pee over the railing," he said, chuckling. "Or don't you pee either?"

"None of your business."

"Anyhow, in that corner will be a navigator's table."

"Who's the navigator?"

"Who?"

Suddenly Alec's impossible dream blossomed into a fantasy of him and her, alone in his beautiful sloop in the middle of the ocean, drifting and loving from tropical island to tropical island. His mustache curved wistfully up at the corners. "The job's up for grabs to anyone who might express an interest."

Planting her fists on her hips, she bent a speculative eye at the area. "I've never had anything to do with boats. What does navigating involve?"

Deviously Alec tried to think how best to win a woman like Bunny over to boating. "The navigator uses tide charts and oceanography maps, plotting routes and sea-lanes, reads the stars with instruments, makes lots of calculations. Nothing a woman with a good brain couldn't learn from a book, or from another experienced sailor."

"Uh-huh! And how did you become so experienced?"

Smiling nostalgically, he ran his fingers through his hair. "One of my college buddies came from a boating family. They used to include me in sailing trips between college terms. Out there on the ocean, nobody depending upon me, I felt young for the first time in my life. So I built a boat of my own with the notion of recapturing the freedom." He quirked one end of his mustache up. "The fantasy keeps me going through all the Woodbox hassles."

"Oh, I almost forgot!" Bunny exclaimed, grabbing his arm. "Speaking of the Woodbox, in all the excitement I haven't told you my wonderful news."

Alec was still sailing on a fantasy. "News?"

"From Cleveland! Your PR expert talked Priceroad into stocking Woodbox kits in all their discount stores!" She clapped her palms on his cheeks. "That's a *big* market, Golightly Man. You've only marketed on the West Coast up to now, but Priceroad has umpteen hundreds of stores from one end of the country to the other."

"Yeah, that's big business, all right," he said gloomily. "But we can't assemble umpteen thousand kits when we don't know if we'll be in existence two months from now. I'm not a bit certain we can raise the down payment before the deadline."

"You aren't seeing the total picture, darling." Bunny curled her arms loosely around his neck. "With a big, lucrative contract like that, we should be able to borrow the money."

He thought for a moment, then whooshed out a breath. "You mean there might be light at the end of the tunnel after all?"

"Looks like it, Golightly Man, and I haven't felt so exhilarated over pulling off a deal in I don't know how long!" she exclaimed, then smiled, her delft-blue eyes softening into a glow. "Except, of course, over my tour through the toy store, but that's in a class by itself."

"You bet it is, Princess!" he said, his eyes glowing right back at her. "And I happen to have champagne waiting in my refridge to toast the beginning of us. Let's go lift a glass in a toast."

"I'd love to, but I don't know if I should," she said, climbing the companionway ladder. "Remember what happened last time I drank a toast."

"The night is branded in my memory," Alec said, eyeing the shapely buns under her shorts. "Be forewarned, I'm not likely to be such a saint if you get potched again."

Stepping out into the night air, she looked back into the hatch, laughing. "I'm actually not all that partial to saints."

It was almost nine when Bunny hopped on her bike the next morning, but she couldn't bring herself to care. Floating on a far downier cloud than the silver ones blanketing the sky, she was barely aware of singing birds, the scent of roses, and the rushing river. Her mind and heart were filled with the touch of Alec's body on hers, his face, his laughter, the joy.

Weaving her racing bike in and out of rush-hour traffic, she felt the giddy urge to smile and wave at the drivers as she passed. It was as if the shackled woman had broken out of prison, and she felt a magnificent sense of freedom.

At the Woodbox, Alec had left a message saying he would be gone most of the day talking to bankers about money. After changing out of her spandex, Bunny went to Packaging to greet the special troop, her morning habit now that Alec was so busy with his managerial duties.

When she entered the assembly room, Tess and Dwight were lying in wait, eager to have a private talk. With glowing, hopeful eyes they asked Bunny if she thought they could have a marriage like real people. Taken totally by surprise, she didn't have any answers for them.

It humbled her even more to make the rest of her rounds, giving each special person a touch and a word. The unquestioning love and trust in their faces led her to understand exactly why Alec felt so pressured to make life secure for them.

By the time she'd made her way back to the business office, Bunny's mind had floated back to her dreamy cloud again. Drifting past Nan with only a smile as a greeting, she sat in the work area she'd created for her stay, using the backup computer. Taking off her glasses, she blew languorous gum bubbles, watching an instant replay of Alec making love to her on the unpowered monitor.

She hardly noticed her office mate setting a cup of black coffee in front of her, then leaning her pregnant body against the table. "Are you sick or something?"

"Hmmm?"

"I'm debating whether I should call the paramedics."

"What?" Bunny gave her gum a loud snap and glanced at the jumper straining around Nan's mountainous belly. "Who needs a paramedic? You're not . . . ?"

"Not me, *you*! I've never seen your head so full of fluff, nor have I seen you in an outfit like that before. What's gotten into you?"

"Gotten into me!" Flustered red spots popped out on Bunny's cheekbones before she realized it was only a figure of speech. She had a fever for sure, but it wasn't the sick kind. "My clothes?" She stared down at her white jeans, blue cotton blouse, and sandals. "I went shopping in Cleveland and bought some things off the rack for the first time in my life. I wanted to look more approachable. I mean, everyone here is so informal and . . . well, you know."

"Mmm-hmm," Nan hummed knowingly.

"I'd better settle down and get to work," Bunny said prudently, not wanting her affair to be common knowledge around the factory.

But not even the computer could distract her. Alec dominated her mind. She'd talked about being happy with the moment, but oh, she wanted so much more. Months, years, forever. Marriage? Unhappily she thought about Dwight and Tess and wondered if she and Alec were any better suited for a long-term commitment. He might be a manager now, but he'd never equal her experience or career potential. She didn't care about things like position and status, but men seemed to feel they had to be dominant.

She'd been left lonely and grieving by tender masculine egos in other love affairs, culminating with Nick. The feeling she felt for Alec was so much more intense. It was unbearable to think of him resenting her capabilities and turning his back on her after the first magic wore off. She'd do anything to prevent that from happening. But what could she do?

Jumping up, Bunny paced the office, stopping at Nan's desk to look at her family picture, including a smiling, ruddy-faced husband. Not willing to reveal her personal dilemma, she went at the subject laterally. "Marriage must be complicated, considering how many end in divorce."

Nan leaned back, lifting her brows questioningly. "I can't argue that."

"Tell me to mind my own business if you don't want to answer, but how do you manage to keep yours happy? Isn't it a problem when your husband is paid hourly and you have a higher position and earn more money?"

"Honey, you opened up a big wiggly can of worms. Chuck's a man's man and thinks a woman's place is in the home. But we couldn't make ends meet without my salary. Sure it makes trouble."

"I was afraid of that," Bunny muttered, letting out a deflating sigh. "How do you handle the problem?"

"All I can do is try to be all woman at home out of respect for his feelings. But even with that we'd be in deep trouble if we didn't know how to talk out our feelings, and maybe laugh at the issues we can't solve."

"I see." Bunny put the picture down and went back to her place at the table, snapping her gum and toying with a pencil. After a bit she mused aloud, "My main problem here is that I never learned to be a woman at all. And neither one of us seems very good at being open." Remembering she'd meant to keep the discussion impersonal, she quickly amended, "This is all theoretical, understand."

"Oh, of course," Nan agreed, shifting her bulk awkwardly in her chair. "But you're making an ocean out of a puddle. Being open is just talking, and being a woman is just catering to your man's primal instincts. Sex, his job, his stomach, and his hobbies."

Turning the pencil end over end, Bunny tried to imagine the look on Alec's face if she should happen to turn into the ultimate woman. Could she pull it off? She glanced at Nan. "Just theoretically, mind you, I have a good handle on the sex end, but I don't know anything about boats, and I sure can't cook."

"Well, shoot, there's a ton of books about boats and twice that many cookbooks. I'm fairly certain you're smart enough to read and follow a recipe." Nan smiled slyly. "Theoretically speaking, the employees are tickled to see that butterfly of an Alec succumbing. They have a pool, betting on how long it'll take him to net you. Gives them something light to think about in these troubled times."

Giving her gum a snap, Bunny threw the pencil down and laughed sheepishly. "Oh, wonderful, just what I needed! Since I can't seem to settle down and get anything done, I might as well go find a bookstore."

In high spirits, Bunny got back into her spandex and took off on her bike to buy a cookbook. After studying a suggested menu, she made several stops on the way to the cottage. Unbagging her groceries in the kitchen, now stocked with hanging copper kettles and African violets on the windowsill, she set about creating a very special evening for her man.

TEN

Alec came back to the Woodbox with exciting news after his banking expeditions. It was disappointing—and surprising—to discover Bunny had left the factory and gone home before noon. Workaholic that she was, the unprecedented event worried him. He hoped she wasn't sick. He shied away from considering the unspeakable, that she might have begun to regret making love and was avoiding him. It would break his heart, because in one heavenly day she'd become vital to his very existence.

He had to shelve his worry until after 6:00 P.M., when he finally finished his duties. Speeding home in his vintage Mustang, he breathed a sigh of relief over seeing Bunny's bike leaning against the cottage. Her Beemer was in the garage when he drove in, proof she hadn't packed up and left.

As he jogged toward the cottage his heart leaped

with happiness when she came out on the porch to meet him. "Why did you leave the office?" he called out. "Are you sick?"

"No, I came home to wait for the lord and master," she called back, grinning.

"But it isn't like you to leave in the middle of the morning!"

"Make up your mind, darling. I recall you were fussing about my working too many hours a while back, now you're fussing about me taking time off."

"Well, Miz Bernice Fletcher, I don't recall you ever following my instructions without a major battle."

"I'm turning over a new leaf," she said, and added, "Don't call me Bernice," though it didn't seem to bother her any longer. She'd begun to feel like a Bernice.

"Bunny, Bunny, Bunny," he crooned, bracing a polished black shoe on the bottom step of the porch.

A breeze out of the sunset whipped the short, flirty yellow skirt around her thighs, catching at the ruffles on a blouse that left her shoulders bare. Her hair was still wet and crimped from a shower, caught back in a ponytail. No glasses, no gum. The sight made Alec feel uneasy for some reason. "Mind you, I love you looking like a cuddly little temptress, but what happened to your power clothes?"

"I've decided to create a new image, Golightly Man," she said, pleased to see that her plot had him looking bewildered and bedazzled.

"Why did you need a new image?"

She held out her arms. "Why don't you come on up here and find out?"

"My pleasure, Princess." Leaping up the steps, Alec enfolded her in his arms and kissed her. "You can't imagine how much I've missed you all day."

"Me, too, darling." She curled her arms around his neck. "That's why I left the office, because I couldn't get anything done for thinking about you."

Gazing down in her face, even more lovely with minimum makeup, he murmured, "I do love coming home to a welcome like this, but I've never imagined myself lord and master of a manor."

"You look incredibly masterful," Bunny said, drawing back to run her hands down the sleeves of his gray suit, pat his blue shirt, straighten his paisley tie. "I can see it in the determination on your face, you're a tycoon out and about town executing major deals."

"That, unfortunately, is what I've been doing," he said, tilting his mustache with a wry smile. "The Woodbox is turning into a damn miniature rat race."

"Go on, you love wheeling and dealing." She touched a fingertip to his rugged, determined features. "I can read your face like a quarterly report."

"Don't get smart with the lord and master," he said, his smile growing into a triumphant grin. "Your friendly neighborhood tycoon talked a bank into matching us dollar for dollar in a loan, if we can raise the first half of the down payment. Beg, borrow, or steal, we ought to be able to do that."

"That's wonderful, darling!"

"You betcha! It calls for a celebration, Bunny Lady. So get back into your power clothes, and we'll go out on the town for champagne toasts and dinner."

Bunny laughed, delighted to have planned her surprise with optimum good timing. "We don't need to go anywhere to celebrate, I've got dinner in the oven and a toast chilling in the fridge—not bubbly, but a good white wine. Come into my cottage, O lord and master."

"*You* made dinner?" He laughed, hiding the fact that his uneasiness had turned into a stir of apprehension. "What did you cook—tofu surprise?"

Bunny's grin froze and faded. That wasn't exactly the reaction she'd been hoping for. Folding her arms over her midriff, she tapped a sandaled toe. "Do we have to go through the same uproar over my cooking as we did over whether I was capable of cleaning the cottage?"

"No, no! I learned my lesson," Alec said quickly, lifting pacifying hands. "It's just that the idea of you slaving over a hot stove came as a surprise, that's all. I have the utmost faith in your abilities."

"Well, I should think so." Her confidence was sheer bravado, because now that he'd sneered, she'd begun to worry about the quality of the meal she'd prepared. Turning, she stalked toward the front door. "It's up to you, come in if you want to."

"I want to, Princess, believe me, I want to."

Alec hadn't been in the cottage since the day Bunny had cleaned. His stirrings of apprehension intensified when he saw she'd added more country, folksy touches. There were embroidered pillows and a granny afghan on the sofa, ruffled gingham pads on a wood rocker, and floral pictures on the walls. White ruffled curtains were tied back at the sides of the windows. In the kitchen, she'd set the table with a blue cloth and checked napkins in flowered napkin rings and candles. The air was filled with a delicious aroma.

He loved the way the cottage looked like a real home, but it was mortally worrisome to see how naturally Bunny had fallen into the domestic life. First housecleaning, now cooking; was the next logical step her wanting babies crawling around her feet?

His heart sank when she began tying on a white ruffled apron. Anxiety made his voice sharp. "An *apron*! What are you supposed to be?"

Her fingers froze on the bow she was building behind her waist. "What's the big deal about an apron?" she asked defensively, hurt and puzzled by his negative reaction.

"I can't understand your obsession for housecleaning and cooking." Unbuttoning his jacket and vest, he pushed his hands in his trouser pockets. "You act as if you're nesting or something."

It occurred to Bunny that he was acting like a butterfly after all, afraid he'd gotten into a sticky situation. She tried to pull her old protective image around herself, but it was difficult in such a flirty outfit. The best she could do was put on the glasses she'd left by the cookbook. "I didn't realize it was an obsession to prepare a meal for a man I like." Her voice was frigid, her blue eyes glacial. "One I *thought* I liked until a few minutes ago."

"No, I didn't mean it that way. I put it badly. The apron got to me. All I mean is that you have too much talent to waste yourself in the kitchen."

"Let me get this straight. Are you saying it's all right for you to play around with a boat, fantasizing about sailing away when life gets tough, but I have to be a dynamic career woman every minute, with no time off for good behavior?" Glancing around her little kitchen, she wondered how her silly little plan could have gone so wrong. Her body sagged as if the weight of the world had descended upon her. "I'm so tired of being onstage and proving myself so you and George can have your dreams come true."

Groaning, Alec pulled his hands out of his pockets and rubbed them over his face. "Oh, my God, you're right, I've been acting like your father! I'm so sorry, sweetheart. You're right, I have been trying to push you into a slot for selfish reasons of my own."

Bunny gazed at him for a few moments. "No, you're right, it's foolish to pretend to be something I'm not. An apron must look ridiculous on me." Reaching behind, she began untying the bow. "And don't apologize, because we both had selfish reasons for going into our love affair. I guess I've just been trying to escape a case of burnout."

Alec put his arms around her and retied the bow

behind her back. "I love you in the apron, Bunny. I love the cottage the way you've done it, and I love the aroma of whatever you have in the oven. I've been acting like a jerk because I'm so afraid I won't fit into your . . . well, your fantasy."

His face was sheened with perspiration and raw with a mix of emotions: fear, yearning, and yes, love for her. Accepting what she saw, rather than what he wasn't saying, Bunny put her arms around his neck. "Darling Alec, you are so dense! My fantasy is having you share my fantasy."

Breath catching, he covered her mouth with a kiss, then lifted his head again. "You've made me very, very happy, sweetheart."

"I'm glad, Golightly Man," she said, smiling. "I hope you're also very, very hungry, because dinner is ready. And I can't guarantee the results, but I'd hate it if all my hard work went to waste. Are you brave enough to give it a try?"

"By now you should know I have a visceral interest in food," he said, lifting a teasing nose for a sniff. "In the discriminating opinion of a junk-food freak, that's a delicious aroma for the tofu you're probably going to sneak onto my plate."

Laughing and relieved that the crisis had, if not passed, been put on hold, she took a chilled bottle out of the fridge. "Here, stop being a smart Alec and open the wine. It's time we had the toast."

"You betcha." He opened the bottle and poured, then

handed her a glass and lifted his own. "Here's to us and the moment."

Clinking her glass to his, Bunny sipped. Thinking about the fiasco she'd created in trying to be a total woman, she wondered if they could anticipate any tomorrows. "Our last few moments have proved being open doesn't come easily. We're still strangers when it comes to understanding each other."

Alec frowned thoughtfully. "Still, it seems to me we took a few significant steps toward knowing ourselves, if not each other. At least I figured out it's not fair to force my expectations on you."

"I tried to manipulate things, too, but only because we're so different, our goals as far apart as the two poles." Toying with the stem of her wineglass, she gave a sad little laugh. "Our case seems about as hopeless as Tess and Dwight's. When I went to Packaging this morning, they asked what I thought about them getting married. They're afraid to bring up the subject to their families."

Alec had been mulling his own wishes for commitment and marriage, and the idea sent his brows shooting up. "What'd you tell them?"

Bunny gave an apologetic grin. "To ask you."

"Thanks a lot!" he said, then sighed. "Yeah, I'll talk to them and feel their parents out about it."

Sipping wine, she looked at his sensual face and virile body. "I knew they were infatuated, but I didn't think about them feeling the same . . . well, you know . . . what we do."

"Only their minds are limited, the other systems work just fine," Alec said, hanging his jacket and vest on a chair back. "But it won't be easy for two people with their limited capabilities to make a life together."

Bunny took a bowl of salad out of the fridge and set it on the table, thinking about how affectionate Tess and Dwight had acted toward each other that morning, and about Nan's marriage. "It seems as if making a relationship isn't easy for anyone."

"I think you're probably right, Princess." Alec sat down in the chair and crossed his knees, twitched his trousers up, and ventured down a more personal path. "Have you ever thought about getting married?"

A wry smile curved Bunny's lips. After the way he'd reacted to her efforts, she wasn't about to tell him she'd planned the dinner around the notion of marriage. "I don't know. I've never thought of myself as very well programmed for marriage. How about you?"

"I'm even less well programmed for it than you, all things considered." Leaning back in his chair, he ran a finger around the lip of his glass. "Ever think of living with a guy?"

"Who doesn't think about things like that?" Slipping new mitts on her hands, Bunny transferred a steaming casserole from the oven to a trivet on the table, glancing sidelong at him. "Why do you ask?"

Drawing in a deep breath, Alec took the plunge in a roundabout way. "Once upon a time I carried Sleeping Beauty into a hotel room, and ever since, I've dreamed of bringing her to my castle and kissing her awake every morning."

Bunny's heart leaped. "Is that an invitation?"

He shifted uneasily. "Sort of. Yes."

After thinking a moment, she sat down on his lap and curled her arms around his neck. "Your castle is very tempting, darling, but Sleeping Beauty is barely finding out who she really is in an ivory-tower cottage. Why don't we leave things as they are for the present, with an open invitation for the prince to come and visit? Often."

Curling his hand around the back of her neck, Alec pulled her face toward him for a kiss. "Be warned, I'm not one to give up. I'll keep hacking away at the brambles until I reach you."

"I'd be disappointed if you didn't." Smiling, she kissed him back. "But if you intend to work so hard, you'd better eat and build up your strength."

Getting out of his lap, Bunny brought two more hot dishes from the oven to the table. Taking off the covers, she served spinach salad, orange-glazed chicken breasts, cheesy broccoli, and brown rice onto their plates. Sitting down, she said nervously, "This is the moment of truth."

"Everything looks interesting," Alec said cautiously, gamely lifting a forkful toward his mouth.

Holding her fork clutched in a fist, she watched with unblinking eyes as he took several bites. If he pretended to like it, his expression would tell the truth.

His face tallied with his words when he exclaimed, "I didn't expect *real* food. This is delicious!"

She gave a weak laugh. "For heaven's sake, did you actually think I'd force tofu on you?"

"It'd serve me right for teasing you." He proved his enjoyment by finishing off the first installment and dishing himself seconds.

Bunny began eating with a hearty appetite inspired by relief and pride. They laughed and talked through the meal, discussing food likes and dislikes. When Alec had forked in the last enthusiastic mouthful and wiped his mouth on a blue-checked napkin, she said slyly, "Did I mention that all my recipes came out of a beginner's healthy-living cookbook? Everything is low-fat."

"I knew it!" he exclaimed, laughing. "You had to sneak something healthy in on me, didn't you?"

"Of course." She leaned her elbows on the table, grinning. "I intend to see that you stay in the fine, prime shape you demonstrated yesterday."

"Oh, is that right?" Alec leaned his elbows on the table, too, letting his warm green gaze caress the breasts hidden under her ruffled blouse. "Since you're so concerned about my body, do you have a really healthy, luscious nonfat dessert planned?"

"There is a certain kind of sweet dish I've become quite partial to," Bunny admitted, eyeing his powerful shoulders and talented hands. "And I do believe the very thought of it has put every cell in my body on alert."

"What a coincidence! Some rather specialized cells

in my body have gone rigidly on alert too." He grinned and moved restlessly. "Should we clear the dishes away and check into that dessert?"

"The dishes can wait right where they are," she murmured.

Grinning, Alec reached out a finger and lightly traced the curve of her ripe bottom lip. "Did you ever read anything so light as fairy tales when you were a kid?"

Bunny nipped the tip of his finger. "I spent lots of time in libraries and read every book of fairy tales I could get my hands on."

"That's the most hopeful thing I've heard about you." Moving his finger to a point lower, he traced the neckline of her blouse. "Then do you have a favorite one?"

"Lately it's been Sleeping Beauty," she said in a husky voice. "But I'll go for any tale Prince Charming starred in. That's who I figured you for the instant you praised my cooking."

Laughing, he got up and pulled her to her feet, nibbling at her lips, brushing his mustache around her face. "Maybe you kissed a frog and didn't notice that nothing changed."

"A prince is still a prince by any other name, Golightly Man," Bunny whispered, looking into his flushed and rugged face. "What's your pleasure?"

Alec's voice was a velvety caress, his eyes tropical green, warming her like a torch. "I feel an urge to play Big Bad Wolf."

"Woo, your urges make me shivery all over." Bunny

gave a throaty laugh. "Little Red Riding Hood has a basket of goodies she's dying to share."

When the alarm buzzed the next morning, Bunny awoke and slapped the snooze button before she realized there was a naked man in bed with her. And she was naked too.

Lifting herself on an elbow, she gazed down at Alec. He looked very young and vulnerable in slumber, lips parted and dark lashes fanned over his cheeks. At the same time he was flagrantly masculine, the sheet pushed down to his waist, baring his furry chest. Awesome muscles bulged in the arms curled over his head. His swashbuckling mustache spoke for itself.

The happiness she felt over having him in her life was beyond anything she'd ever experienced. She refused to listen to a niggling warning deep in her mind that nothing was real. Wasn't it about time she lived out a fantasy? Her life had been too driven and logical up to this point. No joy.

Dipping her head, Bunny kissed him gently on the lips. "Rise and shine, sleepyhead. Time to go to work."

First Alec contracted his muscles in a fascinating awakening stretch. Then he opened his eyes and looked up with a depth of feeling that blanketed her in warmth. "Morning, pretty lady," he whispered, bringing his arms down to cradle her face between his hands. "Am I dreaming, or are you really here in bed with me?"

"If it's a dream, I hope I never wake up."

A smile curved his mustache and he put a hand behind her neck to pull her down for a kiss. When it ended, he whispered, "Last night was the most wonderful in my life, sweetheart."

"Mine, too, darling." Bunny nestled her face on his shoulder, playing a finger through the curly hair on his chest. "What was Sleeping Beauty's name? Aurora? You woke her up good and proper to a world of magic with your loving."

Wrapping his arms around her lithe body, he sighed. "I wish last night could have lasted forever, going on and on, never ending."

They both jumped when the snooze alarm went off again. Bunny pulled away to shut it off. Alec glanced at his watch and groaned. "Next time you dream up a fantasy, how about one where we don't have to get up and go to work?"

"Hopefully with enough practice I'll get it down pat."

"Pat," he whispered, doing just that with a hand on her hip.

Then his eyes slid sideways to look at her. His hand wandered up from her hip to fondle her breasts, then under the sheet to excite the rest of her body. "Isn't it a shame we don't have more time to find out if the wolf has the strength to be big and bad after partaking of a night of goodies."

Flaring into a fever of desire, Bunny laughed teasingly and flicked a finger at the tent pole under the sheet.

"From where I'm lying, the wolf looks amazingly big and bad. And since you're the boss, you don't have to explain why you came in late to work."

Lifting his lip in a fierce, wolfish snarl, he growled, "Let's have another look at those goodies, Red Riding Hood, sweetheart."

Turning on his side, Alec covered her mouth with his, nibbling her lips, entering with his tongue. Coming up onto his knees, he tantalized her nipples with his lips and teeth, brushed her skin with his mustache.

"Love me, Golightly Man," Bunny whispered harshly, her hands eager on his body. "Love me again."

"Yes, I want you, Princess," he whispered, his voice husky.

Joined as one, they played out the ancient dance until Bunny felt herself swept away in desperation for release. Finally she grasped his arms and cried out in a towering climax.

Moments later Alec moaned and shuddered with his own release. Softly, gently, he drifted back down to earth and smiled at her, his eyes filled with wonder. "Pretty lady, you're fabulous. I want you in my arms tomorrow, and all the tomorrows after that."

Bunny put her fingers over his lips. "Shh, let's not think about tomorrows. Let's live moment by beautiful moment."

He kissed her fingertips. "But after this night I'm going to be awfully lonely, by myself in the castle."

Bunny thought for a moment, then smiled down at

him. "I'll have to admit it was wonderful being awakened with a kiss this morning."

"If I remember correctly, the princess woke the prince with a kiss this time, sweetheart," Alec murmured, his voice velvety with loving.

"Does it make a difference?"

"No." He touched the tip of her nose with a finger.

"Good, because I think I'd like to have the prince sleep in my ivory tower every night."

"Well, what an interesting idea, Princess." Wrapping his arms around her, Alec kissed her lips, then he lifted his head. "Why the change of heart? Last night you refused my invitation."

"I know, but moving into the big house would be real life," she said thoughtfully, then smiled. "This is the cottage, the ivory tower, a perfect place to carry on a little fantasy. What do you think?"

"I think you're absolutely right." Alec pressed his face into her hair, grinning like a fool in his happiness. After a few moments he plunged in recklessly and whispered, "I love you, little red Sleeping Beauty."

Bunny's heart leaped with happiness over hearing him say it, even if it was in play. "I love you, too, big bad Prince Charming."

Kissing his sweaty shoulder, she hoped love wasn't the biggest fantasy of all.

ELEVEN

Alec began living in a limbo between the elegant graystone house where he didn't feel at home and the cottage that was a symbol of Bunny's metamorphosis from a dynamic career woman to a sweet gentle homemaker. Gradually his clothes dribbled their way into her closet, his razor and other necessities into her bathroom.

As the days went by, drifting through July, they wandered about in a daze of happiness, laughing, joking, playing in a world of make-believe. They swam in the pool, shared the chores and the cooking, ate in first one house, then the other, but always sleeping in the cottage. It was a seductive, loving dream life. To Alec it seemed they were playing house like a couple of kids.

He wanted their fragile relationship to last, but time was running out. If they didn't have the down payment by the end of August, they'd lose the Woodbox. Either way, Bunny's contract ended soon after. The specter of her other, real life, epitomized by Faline, hung over him like an ax. With the end in view, he still couldn't bring himself to propose marriage, because that would necessitate revealing the ignoble truth about himself. That he couldn't give her the full life she was coming to want as a woman.

As often as their demanding Woodbox schedule allowed, they worked together on the cabin of the sloop. As part of Alec's campaign to convince Bunny to stay, he installed the navigator's table first and filled the drawers with sea charts and maps, a compass and a sextant. It gave him hope when she began studying books on navigation with obvious fascination. One evening he finished installing the built-in table and benches. "There, how about that?"

Putting her glasses down on the chart table, Bunny got up and came over, glowingly tanned in white shorts and a halter top. "It's as cunning and cozy as the table in the cottage. I love it." Blowing an admiring gum bubble, she sat down on a bench and shifted her legs back and forth under the table. "Comfortable too."

Basking in her praise, Alec sat on the opposite bench, leaning on his elbows. "You've been studying those books for a couple weeks now, have you decided where we're sailing to first?"

"I haven't considered the where, just the how." She linked her fingers with his. "Where would you like to go?"

He gazed at her face, as flawlessly lovely with only

a touch of lipstick and eye shadow as with a full complement of makeup. "That's not a hard choice. Tahiti. Ever since I met you, I've been picturing you basking on a pure white beach with foamy breakers rolling in from an azure ocean. You'd have a cinnamon-scented flower tucked behind your ear and you'd be wearing a sarong."

"That sounds heavenly." Bunny gazed at the black T-shirt hugging his shoulders. "And what would you be wearing?"

"I hadn't thought about me, just you," he said. "What would you like me to be wearing?"

A smile twitching her lips, she murmured, "A flower behind your ear."

"Ah-*hah*! If that's the way things are going to be, I'd better hurry up and get this boat done." Alec lifted her hand and kissed her fingers. "Have you ever traveled out of the States, gone overseas anywhere?"

"Not on a boat, and not to Tahiti, but George took me to Europe several times."

The mention of her father brought her crashing down out of the dreamland clouds. Trying to erase him from her mind, she got up and looked into the area where the galley would be, nothing but tag ends of wires and pipes now. It didn't work, she couldn't stop thinking about the life she'd lived before. "George wanted me to have a chance to evaluate different filming techniques. I watched a movie being filmed in Italy, another in France, and some BBC things in England."

Grimacing, he wished he hadn't asked. "Trust George to get maximum mileage out of a vacation."

"Yes, he tends to do that." Bunny wandered back to the navigator's table. "But to be perfectly fair and honest to him, I found the moviemaking process to be fascinating and enjoyed those trips very much." She looked ambivalently back at Alec. "There's no getting around the fact that films are my avocation as well as my profession."

His heart sank. "Maybe, but I didn't particularly want to hear you remind me just now. My fantasy was being on the boat, you and me, no George, no movies."

Bunny came back and put her arms around his shoulders, pressing her face into his crisp, clean hair. "I hope it happens, darling."

"It will, Princess." Praying he was right, he put his arms around her waist.

Though aware he'd closed his eyes to reality, Alec was happy being with Bunny almost twenty-four hours a day, every day, at work and at home. Since she seemed equally blissful it was impossible to hide their fascination for each other from the employees. They didn't even try any longer.

On a Friday he was sitting in the cafeteria, munching a bologna sandwich and drinking a cola. Bunny was beside him, spooning plain yogurt sprinkled with cereal nuggets and sipping mineral water. She'd been out on a marketing tour, and Alec thought she looked too beautiful to bear, wearing a black suit, a starkly tailored white blouse, and gold jewelry. His career woman was back again, and all was right with the world.

It seemed a rude interruption when Jack Budd, head of Maintenance, walked up and sat down at their table, taking his yellow hard hat off. "You know that pool we got going over how long it'll take you two to admit what all of us know already?" he said, his eyes twinkling. "Well, we all decided the winner is obligated to put the proceeds into the pot for the down payment."

"Oh, izzat right?" Alec muttered, twitching his mustache. Beside him, Bunny gave an embarrassed snort of laughter.

"Yep, and we'd appreciate it if you'd let us know the minute something solid develops." Jack gave a wink. "This relationship of yours is a damn cliffhanger, with so much pending, you know?"

"I know," Alec agreed, wholeheartedly.

Jack peered up at the six-foot fake thermometer mounted on a wall in the cafeteria to give everyone a blow-by-blow view of how close they were to raising the necessary funds. "I suppose you also know the money was building up pretty good at first, but it's slowed down lately."

"The fact has entered my mind a time or two." Alec took another bite of his sandwich, scowling at the red line that had become stuck so close to the top. "We're eighty-seven percent of goal, which is a lot closer than we were a few weeks ago."

Jack nodded. "That's true, but the rank and file are beginning to think the last thirteen percent is impossible. None of us working slobs can scrape up anything more to throw in. We're all wondering if you have some plans on how to boost the mercury up the tube."

"Both Bunny and I are making the rounds looking for money."

"We all know that," Jack said, nodding. "But in case you don't come up with something, we been talking among ourselves and thought up an idea for raising funds. I've been elected to run the idea past the business lady there."

Bunny put down her water and lifted her brows encouragingly. "What is your suggestion?"

"Most of us go to churches and clubs around the area, and we were wondering if it'd be legitimate to raffle off Woodbox kits to bring in some extra money, maybe push that mercury up the tube."

Putting aside her yogurt, she sat back, giving him her complete attention. "I've never experienced anything like a raffle, so I'd have to talk with the corporate lawyer about the legal pros and cons before I can make a judgment." She turned to Alec. "What do you think?"

He scratched his head, then swept his hair back into place. "With due respect to our meticulously manufactured product, do you honestly think many people would pay money for a ticket to win an article of furniture they have to put together themselves?"

Jack leaned back in the chair and shoved his hands

in his jeans pockets. "I should think anyone with a house could use a utility cabinet for the garage. But putting that aside, I believe the people in this area might buy a ticket for the hell of it, just to help the Woodbox out." When he grinned, his worry creases deepened. "Especially if the pretty PR business lady went around and asked them. Who could say no to you, Miz Fletcher?"

Bunny took off her gold-framed glasses and cocked a brow at him. "Why, you sweet-talker, you. I do believe you're the one who knows how to talk a woman around. Okay, get me a list of churches and clubs, and if I find out it's kosher, I'll feel them out."

After Jack left, Bunny threw away the remains of her lunch and left the cafeteria. It had begun raining, so she ran at full tilt toward the main building. "Things are not going very well today," Alec panted, running beside her, holding his tweed sport jacket over her head like an umbrella.

"Frankly," she said, ducking inside the door, "I don't recall anything going well at the Woodbox, not once since I came."

"Come in the office so we can have a powwow and reconnoiter the situation."

Hanging his damp jacket on a hanger, Alec rolled his white shirtsleeves up and sat down in the chair he continued to call the seat of very minor power. "Jack's right, we've only got a month left and we don't have our half of the down payment. Do you happen to know the procedure for robbing a bank?"

"No, that isn't my field of expertise, I'm afraid." Bunny sat gracefully on the chair in front of the desk and crossed her slender knees. "How about selling shares to the public?"

"Only as a last resort. I'd hate letting any pieces of the factory slip out of our fingers, or worse, let someone grab up a controlling interest." Alec stared at the duplicate down-payment thermometer mounted on his office wall. "Think selling raffle tickets might bring in any appreciable money?"

"Get real, Golightly Man, you're clutching at straws. How much money could something so limited and trivial bring in? I went along with Jack because it gives the employees hope when they can see things aren't looking good."

"Thanks, I needed the encouragement," he grumbled, making a face at her. "When things begin to go wrong, they generally go in threes. Number one, we've lost the trust of the rank and file, and two, it's raining. I'm waiting for the third shoe to drop."

"Be patient, things will probably work out," Bunny said, unwrapping a stick of gum. "Nothing dire is going to happen."

Just then the intercom blared. "Nan wants to see you, Alec."

"Didn't I tell you? There goes the third shoe," he muttered, pressing the button. "Send her in."

Nan waddled in. "Am I interrupting something?"

"No, just a wake." Alec waved to a chair. "Sit down and take a load off. What's up?"

"I'd just as soon stand, thanks. It's too hard to get up again. My doctor said I'm farther along than we thought, and my blood pressure is a little high. I thought I had another two weeks to train a girl from the pool to take over until I come back, but he wants me to stay home and keep my feet up. I hate doing this to you, but—"

Alec cut her off with a lifted hand. "Not another word, Nan. Your well-being is more important than the damn business office. You're on leave of absence, starting right now. We'll handle things until you come back again."

Bunny got up to bend over Nan's front with a hug. "Don't worry about a thing, I'll take over and train someone," she said, then stood back. "But I'll expect you to repay me by letting me know the instant you have the baby, day or night. Okay?"

"Okay, I promise. Thanks, you guys." Nan grinned slyly. "If the shoe is ever on the other foot, I'll return the favor."

Running his fingers through his hair, Alec muttered an unintelligible comment, ending with, "Damn shoes, dropping like flies."

As soon as she had left, Bunny cried out, "Oh, this is so exciting! I've never held a baby in my arms before. Do you suppose Nan will let me?"

"I shouldn't be surprised, since women have a passion

for passing the little bounders around." Alec drummed his fingers on the desk, trying to think how he could explain his specific problem to a woman who might possibly soon develop an urge for motherhood.

As if to rub his problems like salt into an open wound, the intercom blared again. "Dwight is out here, Alec. He wants to talk to you."

He sat up straight and glanced at Bunny, his brows rising in surprise. "He's never come here before. What do you suppose he wants?"

"Why don't you have him come in and tell you?"

He pushed the button. "Send him in."

Dwight plodded into the office and planted himself in front of the desk, a short stocky man of twenty-five years. Though he was not as retarded as some, his face was marked by Down's syndrome. He looked pleadingly at Alec, his eyes overflowing with tears, words tumbling out. "After you talked to Tess's and my folks, I thought we would get married. I worked it out so we can live in a place where people watch out for us. We get money from the Woodbox to buy what we need. I can figure change and everything. But her folks changed their mind. They told me, stay away from Tess."

"Oh, man, that hurts, doesn't it, buddy?" Alec came around the desk and put an arm around Dwight's shoulders. "They're very protective of her, so don't get your hopes up, but I'll talk to them again if you want me to."

"Thank you, Golightly Man." Dwight's face flooded

with gratitude. "I'll tell Tess you're going to fix every-thing."

As soon as the door closed behind him, Alec clenched his fingers in his hair, groaning. "I can't fix everything! I can't even fix my own problems! Why do they always think I can work miracles? Don't they know I've got feet of clay?"

Bunny put her arms around his neck. "All you can do is your best, you can't change the world."

He sighed. "Four shoes have dropped now. There can't be any more, can there?"

The words were no sooner out of his mouth than the intercom blared again. "Alec, if Miz Fletcher is in your office, she has a phone call."

He pressed the button. "Yeah, she's here and she's got it."

She picked up the receiver, said hello, then, "Why, George, it's such a surprise to hear from you!"

Alec sat down at the desk again, dismally listening to the conversation, mostly one-sided on her father's end.

Hanging up, Bunny said, "George says he misses me so much he's decided to fly up tomorrow and spend the day in a visit. He'll leave on the red-eye again." Her face tightened. "The three months' grace Faline gave me are nearly up, so I imagine he intends to pressure me to accept her offer."

"It must be one of Murphy's laws. No matter how good a fantasy is, reality will eventually rear its ugly head." Alec scrubbed his hands over his face, suspecting his happy new life was hanging on a fraying string. "I guess I'd better go home and begin clearing all traces of me out of the cottage."

Before leaving the office, Alec called Rosie, a less afflicted special person, housecleaner, and talented cook, who cleaned his big house weekly. Luckily she was free the next day to come in to prepare and serve a dinner. Then he and Bunny went home to tackle the cottage.

An hour later he was standing in the small bathroom, clothed in a faded red tank top and old jeans that had been slashed off at midthigh. Tossing his personal items into a box, he had a gloomy premonition he'd never move back into the cottage again.

Bunny had on cutoff jeans and a tank top, too, but hers were new from a store. Standing in the bathroom doorway, she smiled over the way Alec crowded the small room with his big body. He looked paradoxical against the violet-sprigged shower curtain and lacy lavender towels.

The sight reminded her of when she'd first come into the cottage, thinking of it as a cozy dollhouse. She couldn't ignore the fact that she and Alec had been living a fairy-tale life in it. She could only wish for magic to make the fairy tale become real.

Soon she would have to make a major decision about the future. But not yet; she couldn't bear to think of all traces of him being wiped out of the cottage yet. Her life would feel too empty. "Put them back, darling," she said quietly.

He glanced back, his brows shooting up. "I beg your pardon?"

"I said, put your razor and after-shave back in the medicine cabinet, and don't take your clothes out of my closet." She straightened her shoulders and lifted her chin, solidifying the decision. "It's idiotic for you to move out just because my father is coming."

Surprised over the last-minute reprieve, Alec plopped down on the fluffy lavender toilet-seat cover, holding his box of belongings on his knees. "You told George about what you've done with the cottage, so he'll think it odd if you don't show him. And when you do, he isn't going to like finding me in bed with you. Figuratively speaking, of course."

"I believe that's his problem, isn't it?" Lifting his box onto the floor, Bunny settled herself on his knees. "All that counts is that I like you being here, Golightly Man, and I want you to stay."

"I like me here, too, Princess." Alec put his arms around her waist, a smile lifting the ends of his mustache. "But considering how worried you were in southern California about whether your father would accept this little old Oregon Woodbox boy, your new attitude comes as a bit of a surprise."

"To be perfectly honest, it does to me too." Frowning, she slipped her arms over his shoulders, clasping her hands behind his neck. "Eccentric as he is, I love

George dearly, and I'm thrilled over his visit. But I learned a lesson from you in our last encounter with him. It's foolish for me to pretend to be something I'm not for him. And heaven knows I'm old enough to make my own decisions now."

"Good for you, Bunny Lady," Alec murmured, happy to hear her taking a major step toward choosing him over the past. "Speaking of age. You know I'm twenty-seven, but you still haven't told me how old you are. What happened to equal rights?"

"Let me show you where they went." Grinning evilly, she pressed the lever of the toilet, creating a maelstrom under the closed seat. "Suffice to say, I'm old enough that I don't need anyone's permission to sleep with you anytime and anywhere I want."

"Suffice to say, you've made me very happy by declaring your independence."

Bending his head forward, Alec kissed her on the mouth, then parted her lips with his tongue and tasted paradise. Slipping his hands up under her blue tank top, he whispered, "Speaking of independence, Princess, would you be interested in working your way through the national holidays, starting with the Fourth of July?"

Bunny laughed softly. "You mean like shooting off fireworks and—" She broke off to gasp over the sensations spreading out from his talented fingers on her breasts. "Yes . . . *yes*, I would!"

"And waving the flags," Alec whispered.

"You think up the most fabulously thrilling ideas, O lord and master."

Reaching down, Bunny stripped his red tank top off with two hands, then waved it over her head and giggled like a kid. Pulling him to his feet, she nuzzled her face in the crisp brown hair growing in a fascinating pattern on his chest and down his stomach in a line. "Firecrackers," she whispered, kissing his nipples.

"Watch it when you play with fireworks, sweetheart," Alec murmured, his breath coming quickly. "They're explosive."

Reaching around in back, he stripped her shirt up, leaving her hair in wild disarray as it came off. After convulsing her into laughter with his sassy hands, he swung her up into his arms and double-stepped down the hall into the bedroom, tootling "I Love a Parade" between his lips, trombone style.

He draped a shirt on each bedpost and swept the comforter off to reveal white sheets with eyelet edges. "Red-and-blue flags, and the field of white. Now let's see about the holiday picnic." Peeling her cutoffs down, he did his vibrating lip trombone against each area of skin he bared and partook of a thrilling picnic.

"You're a crazy man," she cried, tangling her fingers in his hair as he knelt in front of her.

"I can do sane and decorous, too, sweetheart," he said in a husky voice, gazing up at her. "Anything you want."

"Sane isn't you, or me." Adding a lip trumpet to his

trombone in a Sousa celebration, she pulled him up on his feet. Stripping him of his shorts, she stood back and laughed. "I see you brought your own flagpole."

Fists planted on hips, Alec looked down at himself. "No, a rocket with a lit fuse, ready for blast-off." Gazing at her, he bathed her face with the warmth and desire in his eyes.

She held out her arms. "My sparklers are sparking and sizzling hot."

He laid her back on the bed and stretched out beside her. As he ran his hands and mouth over her svelte, spectacular body, his lovemaking was wild and intense. She matched his fervor with equal desperation, as if they could hold off the inevitable with passion.

The fireworks finale rocketed them up. In the sweet afterglow, he held Bunny in his arms, her body pressed against his, her head on his shoulder. "I love you so much, Princess," he whispered into her tumbled mass of golden hair.

"And I love you, darling." She played her fingers over his muscles, each one so familiar and dear now. The satiny texture of his skin and each scar seemed a part of her. Moving her head, she gazed at his face, loving the flattened nose, square chin, and thick-lashed, gentle eyes. "I felt so lonely when I first came to the Woodbox," she said. "I felt as if I had a huge gaping hole inside, and I was chained in prison in it. Does that sound insane?"

"No, because I've felt that way too." Frowning over

the emptiness of his pre-Bunny era, he caressed her sweaty shoulder. "Or maybe we're both nuts."

"Which makes us very well matched." Lifting her head, she looked down into his eyes. "But you always act like you know exactly who you are and have your life perfectly mapped out."

The ends of his mustache twitched up in a wry smile. "It's all show. It's my choice to work with special people like my sister, but that doesn't mean it was easy giving up everything. I lived through a lot of regret after I turned down an offer to take the Woodbox over, long before you came along. In a little compartment of my mind I was glad the crisis arose and gave me a second chance at the position."

"Yes, I can understand how you must have felt," Bunny said. "And I'm glad you finally trust me enough to share your feelings and sacrifices. It's like a milestone in our relationship." Studying his serious face, she said wistfully, "There are so many important ways to work with the retarded. You don't have to stay in a place that isn't satisfying to you."

Alec gazed back, knowing what she was asking. "If it were just me, I'd think about going down south with you, but I've made a commitment to my Woodbox people. They've so vulnerable and trusting, I can't up and turn my back on them, especially now when things are changing."

"I would have been disappointed if you'd said anything different," Bunny said sadly. "I wish I understood me as well as you understand yourself. All I know is the emptiness in my life disappeared the first time we made love."

"My world was just as lonely, Princess." Alec kissed her on the nose. "And it'll be even bleaker when you leave again."

"When I leave . . . if I leave." Bunny quickly looked around the little bedroom she'd decorated so warmly, and then for several moments gazed into Alec's face. "You know, Golightly Man, my chains fell away when I followed my instincts and came back to the Woodbox. Well, actually, I came back to you, though I wasn't about to admit it then. As tempting as Faline's offer is, it seems as if I'd be a fool to go back and lock myself in a pressured dungeon again. I think . . . yes, I do want to stay here with you."

"Oh, Lord, you don't know how happy I am to hear you say that, Princess, sweetheart." Gathering her against him, Alec felt rockets of excitement and joy shooting through his system. He kissed her face, nose, eyelids, chin, mouth. Then he sighed deeply, frowning. "But what if in the light of reality you regret giving up Faline?"

"Maybe I will reget my decision someday . . . who knows? But I think I'd regret leaving you more." Laying her head on his shoulder, she played with the hair on his chest. "I've jumped into a new program now, and I have to feel my way. On thing I know for certain is that I want to be a woman for you. I'll worry about regrets when tomorrow comes."

Alec cuddled her closer. "All I can do is pray tomorrow never comes."

Smiling, she tweaked a damp curl. "Tomorrow is going to bring George with it. We'd better get up and brace ourselves for him."

TWELVE

Shortly after noon the next day Bunny drove her Beemer to the airport. Despite her stand for independence, she felt herself tightening up like a drum. She dreaded her father's reaction to her decision to stay with the Woodbox and become involved with a man with no future: at least none in George's eyes. She wasn't chewing gum either, knowing he disapproved. It was difficult to throw off the old habit of pleasing him.

Emerging from the portal, George looked as dignified as always in a blue suit, his dark hair waving back from his forehead, going white at the temples. His face lit up when he saw her. "I've missed you, pet," he said, taking her in his arms.

"I missed you too," she said, pressing her face into his shoulder, breathing in his familiar scent. Torn between loving him and fighting the habit, she drew away and stiffened her spine. "Let's go find the car. I can hardly wait to show you Alec's house and the cottage, and the Woodbox."

"Hmm," George commented obliquely. "How nice."

She guessed he wasn't thinking nice at all, and her nerves tightened up a few more notches. Gripping the wheel with white-knuckled fists, she initiated the justifications she had prepared. "I know you will probably think this is strange, but I've begun to love this area, and now I'll show you one good reason," Bunny said as she merged the Beemer onto a freeway that was practically deserted by Los Angeles standards. "And there's no smog, did you notice?" At least not on the weekend.

George didn't seem impressed.

Beginning to feel defensive, she glanced out over the beautiful city, surrounded by forested hills, dominated by rivers and a peaked, snowcapped mountain. "There's a fabulous Japanese garden and fantastic rose gardens up in a park on those wooded hills across town. Portland is the City of Roses, did you know? The twin glass-paned pinnacles over there are the new convention center. The creators must have been men, because they didn't think of how anyone could wash the windows."

"Hmm," George observed, watching her sidelong with puzzled eyes.

Glancing back, Bunny felt certain there was more involved in his visit than missing her. She didn't look forward to a confrontation over her decision not to go with Faline. Especially when she was fighting her own mixed feelings about it. Forestalling the inevitable, she jumped back into a travelogue that bored even her.

"Hmm" was all George said when she finished. He was studying her with open curiosity.

She knew her babbling had made him suspicious, but she didn't think his *hmm*s boded well either; he was generally more verbal. "We're in the state of Washington now," she said, turning eastward, and then into the driveway; she parked in front of the big graystone house. "And here we are."

"Good Lord, *this* is Alec Golightly's house?" George exclaimed, shocked into an impressed reaction despite himself.

Prickling with relief, Bunny said, "Yes, he inherited it. His father was an extremely successful lawyer until his death. Harvard, you know. You can see the boat Alec is building over the end of the garage roof."

He gave a more speculatively interested *hmm* over the boat.

They climbed out of opposite sides of the car. Bunny noticed George watching with increasing interest as she straightened her short knit skirt and matching pink top, and smoothed her curly hair back into the ponytail that she'd come to find easy to wear. Smiling nervously at the expression on his face, she hoped her new image wasn't too much of a shock for his heart. "Come in and let me show you the house."

He didn't comment on her clothes, but he did lift a

questioning brow at the house. "I thought you lived in the cottage."

"I do," she said, waving a hand toward the miniature graystone where Alec was waiting. They had agreed it would be better if she announced her living situation before the two men encountered each other. She hoped she could get a mellowing drink into George's hand before the subject came up.

Walking up on the porch of the big house, Bunny led him through the front door. Continuing to delay the inevitable, she led him on a tour. He walked without comment through the foyer and down the long hallway, in and out of large rooms, *hmm*ing over her commentary. She ended the tour in the living room. "What do you think?"

"It is a lovely house, but it has a deserted feeling," he answered with perspicacity. "As if no one was living here."

"It's not deserted, there's a woman in the kitchen preparing dinner." She smiled wryly. "We're ordinarily so busy, we live very simply, but we're putting on the dog and going formal for you."

"Hmm," he answered, lifting a suspicious brow.

"Would you like a drink, George?" she asked, seating him on one of the couches.

"A scotch on the rocks would be most welcome," he said, as if he needed one badly.

Pouring drinks from a wet bar hidden in a massive limed-oak wall unit, she handed him his scotch and sat down beside him, sipping wine. "I can't put it off any longer, George," she said, setting her glass on the table. "The house has a deserted feeling because Alec moved out. He's living with me in the cottage. We've fallen in love."

Her father took a quick gulp of scotch, the ice cubes rattling loudly before he said, "Yes, I expected as much."

Bunny's lowered brows shot up. "You did?"

"How naive do you think I am, pet?" he asked aridly, a corner of his mouth quirking up. "I've lived in one of the most sophisticated areas of the world for a very long time."

Bunny laughed sheepishly. "Alec offered to move out of the cottage while you were here, so it's a good thing I didn't let him. It would have been an insult to everyone's intelligence."

"Yes, I should think so." He took another swallow of scotch, as if strengthening a resolve. "Are you absolutely certain this is what you really want, Bunny?"

"Yes, I'm sure." Thrusting her chin forward, she geared herself to stand up to his disapproval. "I'm happier than I've ever been in my life since I came back to Alec." Taking a deep breath, she presented the rest of it. "It hasn't been an easy decision, but I'm going to stay and make a new life here with him."

"I know you've been under stress for a long time, pet, and struggling over the direction of your career," George said, looking suspiciously like he'd bit into a persimmon. "I understand you love Alec, but is love enough to satisfy your gifts and talents?"

After a thoughtful hesitation she answered, "Believe it or not, I've become very attached to the special people and the Woodbox. That and Alec are enough."

Her father managed a weak smile. "Then I'm very happy that you've finally discovered what you want in life."

A few silent moments stretched as Bunny stared at him in disbelief. "That's it? But I expected an apoplectic fit like you had over my putting Faline off and coming up here. At the very least some of the ice you dished up when I brought Alec to meet you. I had bundles of justifications prepared."

George winced and smiled wryly. "One of the reasons I came to visit is to apologize for interfering too heavy-handedly in your life. I'm somewhat belatedly cutting you loose. You know far better what is right for you, and I wish you good fortune in your choices." The persimmon puckered his mouth again. "Even if it happens to be the Woodbox."

His visit was becoming very curious, but Bunny wasn't about to analyze her good fortune. She felt a wash of relief and gratitude over his approval. "I seem to have been underestimating you," she said, bending sideways to give him a hug.

"No, you haven't, pet, I've made serious mistakes in your upbringing." George glanced at her simple, feminine clothes, then up at her fresh, minimally made-up face. "I suspected when you arrived with Donald Duck on your head. I had never seen you look so happy and free before. Alec drove the fact home by telling me I hadn't taught you how to have fun. He's right, and that's a very sad statement about a father. I loved you, but I wasn't a good parent."

Bunny had never heard him admit to making a mistake before, and half wondered if he might be having a mental breakdown. "George, are you all right? You aren't sick?"

"No, my health is excellent. Why?"

"I don't understand this transformation in you."

A wry smile curved his finely chiseled lips. "Have I been that overbearing?"

"Just remember you brought up that word, not me."

Laughing, Bunny got up and held out her hand. "Let's go say hello to Alec at the cottage. And then I'm going to give you a tour around the Woodbox, whether you want one or not."

Bunny had planned the dinner, served at seven that evening, which meant it was far more graciously done than if Alec had had his junk-food hand in it. She'd gotten out all the niceties his father had gathered during his residence, and the table glowed with candles, white linen, fine china, sterling silver, and a bouquet of roses from the garden.

Rosie may not have been as sharp as a tack, but she had a gifted touch in the kitchen. It tickled her to wear a black-and-white maid's uniform while serving a summer-lettuce salad, salmon stuffed with wild rice, baby peas, and assorted side dishes.

The presentation clearly impressed George, and his manners were as elegant as always. If he had shell-shocked opinions about his daughter being in a relationship with the man at the foot of the table, he kept them to himself.

Alec looked stylish in a gray jacket, a black shirt, and a wildly flowered tie. Pouring a fine French wine, he kept a grin hidden under his mustache. Bunny knew he thought the situation was hilarious.

Praying neither of her men would lose their grip and cause a scene, Bunny presided at the head. She'd dug into the back of her increasingly informal closet for a slim white sheath that left her shoulders bare and made her tan glow. In her heart of hearts, she found a formal dinner a nostalgic treat after several weeks of do-it-herselfing in a dinette.

To her surprise, George acted more human than usual and had them almost in tears, laughing over gossipy stories from his years in promotion. Even more astonishing, he seemed interested in Alec's tales of derring-do from his sailing adventures. "I didn't know you were interested in boats," she said, pushing her glasses up on top of her head.

"Didn't I tell you I used to love to sail when I was young?"

"No, you certainly did not!" she exclaimed, trying to picture her father sailing off into the ocean.

After sipping wine, he said negligently, "I once was a crew member in the Australia Cup competition."

Alec's opinion of George escalated several notches. "Racing for the Aussie Cup is one of my wildest dreams!"

"Unfortunately we lost." Leaning back to let Rosie remove his empty plate, George smiled up at the woman. "A wonderful dinner, my dear," he said in a gentle voice. "I haven't eaten a finer meal anywhere in the world."

Ducking her head, Rosie blushed furiously with pleasure and hurried back to the kitchen. Bunny couldn't believe her father had said something so sensitive and kind. "I'm beginning to think I don't know you at all, George."

He smiled almost playfully. "Do children ever know their parents?"

Alec laughed. "Seems like I recall my mother saying something like that."

Rosie served key lime pie and coffee, then hustled out again. Alec opened a bottle of dessert wine and brought up his favorite subject again as he poured. "Why did you quit sailing, sir?"

"The pressures of a demanding profession didn't leave me time." George patted his lips with a napkin. "My wife wasn't interested in boats. I preferred being with her."

He'd never volunteered information about her mother before, so Bunny quickly leaped in to ask, "What was she like? You loved her very much, didn't you?"

"She was a beautiful, vivacious woman, and yes, I adored her." He studied Bunny for a moment, then toyed with his coffee cup, looking down. "She shared her name, Bernice, with you and also her extremely powerful intellect."

Apprehension suddenly speared through Alec, a feeling of lead dragging his stomach down. Pushing his untasted pie aside, he leaned forward on his elbows. "How did Bunny's mother use her gifted mind?"

George gazed intently at the younger man. "She didn't develop it, unfortunately. When she was young, a woman went to college to find a good husband, not to make use of her own intellectual gifts. She was happy for the first year or so, but a husband, a home, and volunteer work weren't enough stimulation. She dreamed of a career, but didn't follow through on her plans. She thought a baby would fulfill her."

"Me," Bunny murmured.

"Yes. She loved us both, but I'm fairly certain she crashed her car into the overpass to escape from a life that wasn't fulfilling. I blame myself for not taking her unhappiness seriously enough." He gazed at Bunny. "That's why I felt it was vitally important for you to develop your mind." He smiled wryly at Alec. "As you pointed out, I overcorrected. I should have let my daughter be a child too."

Sobered by the story, Bunny wondered if her mother had felt like a chained woman also. "How odd. I've had the education and opportunities my mother wanted. And here I am, pining for what she had—a home and a family." She glanced apologetically at George. "Despite your

protests to the contrary, I know you must be disappointed that your dream of Faline for me isn't coming true."

"Exactly. The dream was mine, not yours." A smile
spread over her father's handsome face when he looked
from Bunny to Alec and back again. Lifting his wineglass
in a salute, he said, "If this is your dream, then I wish you
both every happiness."

They drifted into other, lighter subjects then. But
worried lines began etching themselves into Alec's forehead as he gazed at Bunny. She was so lovely in the
candlelight, so brilliant, dynamic, and ambitious in a
designer dress. In the depths of his heart he couldn't help
wondering whether she'd go the route of her mother
if she buried herself in a life without stimulation and
challenge.

As the days flew by, Bunny decided it was darned
lucky she felt stimulated by making a home, because the
Woodbox wasn't the epitome of a scintillating career.
She'd been making the local rounds, publicizing the
Woodbox problem and organizing raffles in employee
churches and clubs and local businesses, hitting up anyone
who wished to participate. She didn't expect her efforts to
bring in enough money to spit on.

A few days after George's visit, she was in Alec's office,
moodily chewing gum and watching him sit behind his
desk, pretending to be deeply involved in some paperwork. She had a fair idea what he had on his mind.

They'd been tiptoeing around the edges of George's revelation, shying away from talking about her mother's death and the implications. Alec's sagging shoulders told her how deeply he'd been affected. Instinctively she knew it would be unwise to admit how bored she was with helping run the business office and the raffle rounds.

Involved in their own thoughts, they both jumped as if hit by an electrical charge when the intercom blared. "Alec, you have a top-priority phone call."

Heart thumping, he grabbed the receiver. "Yeah, this is Golightly." He listened for several minutes. "Hey, that's great, man. Congratulations."

There was a taut, anxious look around his eyes when he hung up and looked at Bunny. "That was Chuck Turner."

"And . . . ?" she exclaimed, holding a palm up, fingers flapping. "And?"

"Nan had the baby. It's a boy."

Bunny let out a whoop. "A boy! Oh, my God, how exciting! I can't wait to see it."

Nan was just as eager to invite them over after she came home from the hospital, more than willing to show off her pride and joy.

After work, Alec set off with Bunny by his side in the Mustang with the top down. The arrival of the baby had sent premonitions of disaster running rampant through his gut.

He glanced at her every few seconds, almost as if reassuring himself she was still there. She was svelte and sophisticated in a mauve suit, gold jewelry. She had her face lifted to the wind, her mane of amber hair blowing in a thousand directions, like sun rays. The solar power of his existence, he thought, smiling slightly. The smile died aborning.

It terrified him to think Bunny might slip into the same trap her mother had if she stayed with him. In his heart he knew he would eventually have to send her away, but his tongue wouldn't form the words.

Hand in hand they walked in the front door of Nan's tract house. Though not fancy or roomy, it was filled with love and noise and happiness. Six-year-old Debra was excited about her new brother. Chuck was handing out cigars; Bunny took one too. Nan's mother was nattering around, trying to bring order out of chaos. Nan was lying on the sofa like a queen, belly under control again in a flowered robe. "Want to see him?" she asked, grinning.

"I can hardly wait!" Bunny cried.

The bassinet had eyelet ruffles to the floor, blue ribbons. As Bunny looked into it all she saw was a lump under a blue blanket and a ball sprinkled with dark hair. Then two arms stretched upward, hands spreading like miniature starfish, proving it was a living creature. "Have you named him?" she asked.

"Matthew," Nan said, beaming. "Want to hold him?"

With fear and trembling, Bunny held out her arms too receive the tiny bundle. After Nan had helped her through an initial awkward juggling, the baby molded into her shape like a piece in a jigsaw puzzle. Holding a mite of life in her arms was like nothing she'd ever experienced. "Imagine the engineering it took to make woman and babies fit so perfectly together," she said, glancing up at Alec with a tender smile on her lips.

"Yeah," he said, standing nearby, hands jammed into his trouser pockets.

"How can a human be so tiny and exist?" Eyes glowing like melted sapphires, she gazed down at the little crumpled face, eyes pinched shut, a button for a nose, round cheeks. "Isn't he adorable?"She looked up at Alec with a soft, teasing laugh. "I want one of these."

"Yeah," he whispered, his heart turning to ice.

Everything he'd ever wanted in life was represented in this room: Bunny, love, family, a place of his own in the world. The smile of yearning and magic on the face of his career woman proved God had built the urge to have babies into all women. He gazed sadly at the infant face, an inch away from her breast. It hurt like a physical wound to know he'd never see his own baby there.

Bunny was still walking on cloud twelve and a half or so when they got home. She changed into a flowered romper and began preparing halibut steaks for dinner. "I still can't believe how incredible it felt to hold a miracle in my arms," she said, glancing back at Alec.

In shorts and a soccer shirt, he was wandering about,

fingering her homey decorating touches. He stopped at the window and batted at a ruffled curtain. "Yeah."

Pausing in cutting a lemon into thin slices, she looked at him. "That's all you've been saying all day. Is the needle stuck in your record or something?"

He made a stab at a sickly smile. "Yeah."

"Smart Alec." Turning back to her chore, she hummed over thoughts stirring around in her mind. Putting potatoes in the microwave to bake, she glanced back at him with a grin. "Has it occurred to you our roles have changed since I came here?"

"How do you mean?" Alec asked, taking a chair at a table already set with place mats and pottery.

"I came in as a dreaded efficiency expert with your fate resting in the palm of my hand," she said, tearing assorted greens into a bowl for a salad. "Now you're the boss, and I've become something of a glorified house-wife."

"Yeah." He sighed deeply, thinking how hard he'd worked to prevent that very thing from happening.

"It didn't occur to me until I held the baby." Bunny began slicing veggies with a French knife. Pausing, she turned her head to smile at him. "Wouldn't it be a kick if we got married and had babies of our own?"

Alec literally jumped, every muscle contracting. He swallowed convulsively. "It'll never happen."

Bunny wondered if she'd heard correctly. Putting the knife down, she turned around. "I don't understand."

He got up and rubbed his cold wet palms on the

front of his shirt. "I told you my sister's retardation was genetic. Hasn't it occurred to you that even if I'm not affected, I have the same genes? I decided I could never take a chance on subjecting a child to a tragedy like that." He swallowed again, though his mouth was dry. "I had a vasectomy before I went out and began spreading sperm around."

"A vasectomy," Bunny repeated, attempting to absorb the full implications.

He pushed his hands into his pockets. "That's right, Princess. I can't give you the babies you want."

His white, tense face told Bunny how difficult the confession had been for him. Pushed by a rush of sympathy, she went forward with her hands held out. "Alec, I don't care about that."

Stiffening, he waved her away. "Don't tell me you don't care. I saw the look on your face when you held the baby earlier. You're too much woman to waste yourself in a sterile relationship."

"Alec, I love you and that's all I need." She pushed past his barrier of hands and put her arms around his waist. "I would not be wasting myself by staying with you."

"I love you, too, sweetheart, so much," Alec whispered, crushing her against his body.

But he couldn't stop George's story about her mother from replaying itself over and over in his mind.

THIRTEEN

In mid-August, Bunny walked into the office in a gray man-tailored pants suit, carrying her briefcase. "I'm back."

"I see." Alec had been sitting in his chair with his brown wingtips up on the corner of the desk, ankles crossed. On the surface he appeared to be sorting through paperwork, but in reality he'd been thinking about his life with Bunny lately. They were still living and loving in the cottage, but a quiet desperation had crept into their relationship. It lifted his spirits a little to see the expression on her face was as delighted as sun breaking through clouds. "What's happening?"

"I'm not absolutely sure whether to be astonished or triumphant," she said, running a red marker up to the top of the thermometer mounted on his wall. Pushing her glasses up on her head, she crossed the office and put her arms around the boss in a long, consuming hug and kiss. Then she boosted herself up onto his desk, sitting next to his legs. "Well, we've reached our goal. We have our half of the down payment, and the bank will match us the rest. The Woodbox is home free."

Flushed and melting with the heat of her embrace, Alec dropped his feet to the floor with a couple of thumps and sat up straight. "You're kidding!"

"Do I ever kid?"

The wheels began spinning in his mind. "But if we're this close to owning the factory, I'd better put the rank and file on double shifts to manufacture the Priceroad commitment. I'll have to hire a bunch of assemblers to help the special troop put together so many kits. Something interesting is going to come out of this operation yet."

"Sure, *lots* of cheap kit furniture," Bunny said, smiling at his enthusiasm. "And to think Jack Budd had to push me into making it possible with raffles."

He gave the concept a wobbly smile. "Is that how you did it?"

"Yes. I couldn't believe it either, but on top of all the tickets that were sold in the churches and local stores, the Woodbox members of the VFW brought in a humongous amount raffling off an entertainment center that isn't worth beans in a store. It's incredible how eager everyone was to support the Woodbox." Snorting a laugh, she unwrapped a stick of gum. "We fast-track types are more accustomed to everyone ripping the next guy apart in the rat race than winning with raffles."

Alec tried to laugh, but the fast-track joke wasn't funny any longer. "It looks like the moment of truth then. We've accomplished what we set out to do, the two of us." He forced himself to say it. "And your three-month hiatus from real life is coming to an end."

"A hiatus!" she repeated questioningly. "I'd call our last three months a little more than that."

Clearing his throat, he knew that now that he'd opened the subject up, he had to go on, for her own good. "I've done a lot of thinking since your father was here and told us about your mother. All I can figure out is that you'd be happier going back home to work with Faline."

Sitting on his desk in front of him, Bunny stiffened over hearing the first rumbles of disaster. She took her gum out of her mouth and dropped it in the wastebasket. "I thought it was all settled. I intend to stay here with you."

"Princess, imagine what the Woodbox is going to be like now that the crisis is over. How long would a woman like you be satisfied in raffleland?"

She began to protest but closed her mouth. Picking up a pewter paperweight in the shape of a sailing vessel, she turned it over and over in her fingers, the corners of her mouth aimed downward, thinking. "Yes, the situation will be very different from now on, but . . ."

Alec jumped up and stalked across the office to stare out the window. It seemed odd for the August weather to be so beautiful and sunny when a tempest of emotions was going on inside him. The idea of sending Bunny away and going back to his old swingin'-single life was as depressing as death. "If I had my boat finished, I could sail in the Australia Cup."

Half-turned, looking toward him, she said, "You aren't sailing into any escapes unless I come along as navigator."

"At the rate we're going, we'd probably end up at the damned South Pole," he muttered, shoving his hands into his trouser pockets.

"So, I look great in fur. Fake, of course, I never wear the real thing," Bunny said, anxiously studying his stiff-spined back.

"That's a fantasy," Alec said, turning to prop his hips on the sill. "Now it's time to face the reality. I've fallen in love with a brilliant, successful woman, and I can't figure out how George could have stood losing your mother that way."

Jumping to her feet, Bunny rushed across the room and put her arms around his waist, burrowing her face into his shoulder. "Oh, Alec, I know. I've been thinking about her too," she said, her voice muffled. "The idea scares me."

"It should, Princess." Pulling her close to his body, he wrapped his arms tightly around her back. "Obviously George didn't take it well, seeing as he never remarried, but think how much worse it was for her, considering that he's still here and she isn't." A moment passed. "I want you to stay with me so badly, but I couldn't bear to watch you spiral down into despair and lose the will to live."

Lifting her head, Bunny gazed at the strength, caring, and gentleness in his face, then pulled out of his arms and drew back to set her high-heeled feet. "I'm not the kind of woman my mother was, Golightly Man. You know I'm not a martyr, having run up against me when things weren't going my way." Her lips trembled into a smile. "I love you. I'll be happy."

"Your mother loved George. And me and the Woodbox aren't half as exciting a package deal as he was." Alec crossed his arms to keep from reaching out to her. "When you first came, I thought a career woman was what I needed to fit into my life, but I didn't take into account that brilliant women require mental stimulation. There's none of that at the Woodbox."

Bunny clamped her fingers onto the bulging biceps of his crossed arms. "Alec, it isn't like Portland is the end of the world. There are other things I can find to do if I happen to get bored."

Wishing he could grasp at straws with her, he sighed. "Bunny, when you came here, you were burned out and going through an identity crisis, very vulnerable. But you can't erase the fact that you've been groomed from childhood for a superstar position in film production. After a few years you'd regret giving up the dream."

"No!" she cried, though she knew there was some truth to his words; her eyes filled with tears. "I suppose Faline's offer might have been tempting if I hadn't met you first. But I did, and I'm not the same woman now. I have other interests. I want a home, and you, and—"

She clamped her mouth shut, but not soon enough; Alec's body went rigid. "Yes, what about those babies you want? The Woodbox can't fulfill your mind, and I can't fulfill that area of your life." Gazing down at her, Alec hated himself for causing tears to course down her cheeks. "Are you willing to give up any chance of becoming a mother?"

"Darling, I—" Bunny began, then hesitated, thinking how sweet and tender little Matthew had felt in her arms.

"I thought so," he said in a choked voice.

"Alec, this isn't fair!" Bunny cried, clenching her teeth against the sobs rising in her throat. "You've thought up major questions to throw at me, and I haven't had a chance to research the dozen or so perfectly logical solutions there must be."

"Don't you think I've thought and thought, lying awake night after night, agonizing over this, sweetheart?" he exclaimed miserably. "There's only one answer. I love you too much to let you stay here and give up everything."

Frozen with dread, she tightened her fingers on his arms. "You're making me feel torn in every direction."

"I am, too, Princess," he whispered, then straightened his shoulders. "You insisted upon a business relationship at first. We should have left it at that. Maybe it'll be easier if we end it that way now."

"I don't know what you mean," she said, gazing up into the roiling sea in his green eyes.

"I mean I'm going to fire you." Shaking inside, Alec peeled her hands off his arms and walked across the room to sit behind his desk. He picked up two papers stapled together. "Here's the contract you signed, agreeing to act as consultant through the Woodbox crisis, or for no more than three months. You agreed in writing that I'm the boss and I make the final decisions. Well, I decree the crisis is over. I'll send your fee in shares as soon as the legalities are finalized. Is that all right?"

"Yes." It seemed as if someone else had agreed in a voice she didn't even recognize.

The next words killed Alec inside. "You might as well go to the cottage and pack your things. The longer you stay, the harder the parting will be."

"The cottage?" Bunny braced a hand against the windowsill, tears pouring down her face as she thought of the love they'd shared, the laughter, the spats, the joy. "I was a fool to think tomorrows weren't important, Golightly Man," she said in a choked voice. "I'll never be able to forget our time together."

Biting into his mustache to stop his lips from trembling, he rubbed his hands over his face. "If you go home and accept the job with Faline, you'll be so busy, you'll forget me in no time."

Rushing across the office and around the desk, Bunny dropped to her knees beside him, putting her arms around his body. "How soon are you going to forget me, darling?"

Alec put his arms around her and rested his face in her fragrant mass of spiraled amber curls. "Never."

"That's when I'll forget you too."

Lifting her chin with his hand, he kissed her on the mouth, then forced himself to draw back. "You'd better go, Princess."

With the brush of his mustache branded on her face, she climbed shakily up onto her feet. Numbly she put on her glasses, picked up her briefcase, and walked to the door. She hesitated a moment, hand on the knob, then rushed quickly out, slamming it behind her.

Alec sat motionless for a long time. The pain he felt was a living thing. Finally he dropped his head down on his crossed arms and wept.

It was heart-wrenching to say good-bye to the special troop. Tess hugged Bunny tightly, weeping copious tears. Dwight glowered in his usual way of expressing emotion. Bunny could hardly bear knowing their love was as hopeless as hers. Jake rocked back and forth, making grief-stricken hand gestures. The others touched her gently, sadness and puzzlement written on their faces. By the time she left, she felt torn into a thousand pieces.

The pieces shredded into a million and blew away in the wind as she walked slowly through the tiny rooms of the cottage for the last time. She touched Alec's razor in the bathroom, his mustache comb. Picking up a T-shirt he'd thrown on top of the hamper that morning, she buried her face in his scent and wept like a lost soul.

The tears stopped finally, but the grief didn't. It was true, she'd been programmed to be a mover and shaker and couldn't erase what she was. But how could she go back to her old life after the Golightly Man had taught her to have fun and play, and to be vulnerable? In throwing off her chains, she'd lost the knack of retreating behind an image to protect herself. She was doomed to face the pain as well as the joy of living.

Unable to bear another minute, Bunny threw her things into suitcases and boxes, dumped her power clothes into a heap in the backseat, and attached her bike to the top of the Beemer. As she drove away from the cottage the tears were so thick in her eyes, she could barely see.

Late in the evening of the second day, Bunny walked into the Beverly Hills house, feeling as exhausted and drained as a zombie. She didn't even have the energy to chew gum. She walked into George's office. He jumped up and gathered her into his arms. "You look terrible, Bunny, absolutely haggard. What are you doing home?"

Drawing away from his arms, Bunny walked across the office to look at a life-size portrait of the original Bernice, eternally young, forever beautiful, so unhappy she'd forsaken the people who had needed her so badly. She turned to look at George. "Things didn't work out between me and Alec."

"I'm so sorry," he said, his face sagging.

For a moment she stood motionless, eyes closed, her core crackling like an ice floe. Then she cried out, "Oh, George, Alec is my whole life, my everything. Why couldn't I have been a different person? Why couldn't his background have been different? Why couldn't we have met in a different situation?"

Her father took her glasses off and folded them into his pocket. Then he gathered her into his arms, holding her tightly. "Let it go, pet, let the pain out."

When the bitter flood of tears had dried up, she sat down in one of his winged armchairs. "At first I thought Alec was a butterfly out to bed a glamorous woman, but he's as far from one of those as a man could be."

George leaned forward in the matching chair, his elbows on his knees, looking up at the portrait of his Bernice. "It is a very rare young man who would love a woman so selflessly, he'd consider her happiness and well-being before his own."

She made a sound in her throat, part sob and part laugh. "I wish Alec had been selfish enough to talk me into staying. I want to be with him, no matter what."

He turned toward her, scowling. "Whatever other mistakes I might have made as a father, I did not bring you up to be a quitter! Go get some sleep so you can think clearly and resolve this foolishness!"

"I can't think when my mind is full of misery over Alec."

Alec was so busy doing double duty, taking care of the business office until Nan could come back, that he only had time to wonder every three minutes or so what Bunny was doing, if she missed him, if she was living it up on the fast track. He was able to devote his full time to being miserable after Henry came back from his Alaskan fishing trip, bored and eager to help out around the factory.

The weekend was terrible. He wandered through the deserted cottage, hearing the echoes of Bunny's laugh, feeling her kiss, seeing her cooking in the kitchen. He looked out the window where she'd loved to stand, gazing at the river and Mt. Hood. He went into the bedroom where they'd loved so many times. The embroidered pillows, flowered pictures, and ruffled curtains that had made it so cozy a home were still there, but the life was gone.

After moving his things back into the big house, he changed into ragged jeans and a faded T-shirt. Climbing the scaffolding to his boat, he knew it was so close to being finished now that he could have sailed off into the wild blue yonder. It was tempting, with the rest of his life stretching before him like a desert.

Climbing down into the cabin, he found a book left out on the navigator's desk, the place marked with a gum wrapper. The space was scented by Bunny's musky perfume. The memory of their first loving was a living thing.

Stumbling back up the ladder, Alec threw himself out onto the deck, lying full-length, gasping. He didn't even have his boat for an escape any longer. Bunny had touched his entire life.

The cottage drew him the way an aching tooth invited the probing of a tongue. Sitting on the couch in the homey, barren living room, he stared at nothing, not even aware of time passing in his pain. A kiss on the cheek brought him back to life. He glanced up, too depressed to feel surprise. "Hi, Mom," he said apathetically.

"Hello, dear, I'm back from Machu Picchu," Frances said. She wore an embroidered Inca blouse and skirt and sandals laced to her knees. "What's wrong, son?"

He sighed, his hands lying limply by his sides. "What makes you think anything is wrong?"

"It has to be when you call me Mom instead of Ma, and you look like death warmed over." Frances glanced around the living room, realization dawning. "You fell in love with Bunny and she left you for Faline, is that it?"

"She didn't want to go, but I made her understand it was the best thing," he said miserably.

Frances sat down on the couch and slipped a comforting arm around his shoulders. "May I ask why you did a ridiculous thing like that?"

Hitching forward on the couch, Alec leaned his elbows on his knees, hands dangling between his legs. Telling her only the bare essentials of the relationship that had flared and died, he glanced up and studied his mother's face as if she had the answer to his heartaches. "Now do you see why I had to send her away?"

"No, I can't say that I do. Why didn't you go down to southern California with her?"

He stared at his hands hanging lifelessly between his knees. "I couldn't leave the troop. You of all people should understand that."

"Alec, I have as much feeling for the retarded as you do. Carol was my daughter, don't forget. But I've managed to work with them without sacrificing my entire life. You act as if you're trying to atone for another man's sins. The troop can adjust to losing you, and you know it."

"Be that as it may, it doesn't change the fact that Bunny wanted a baby and I can't give her one."

"Son, you are making me so impatient!" Frances gave his arm a shake. "When are you going to let go of the past and grab on to the present?"

He sighed again, nothing sinking in. "It's too late. Bunny's probably under contract and busy working for Faline."

Bunny watched Faline's films over and over on the VCR. The producer-director was a talented feminist with enough sensitivity to play out the problems of ordinary women in her films. Bunny admired her enormously. After thinking until she thought her head would burst, she finally knew what she had to do. Clutching the telephone receiver in a fist, she said, "It's an honor to be invited to work with you, but I can't accept your offer."

The response came crackling over the wire. "Oh, fudge, I suspected this would happen if I let y'all go up north to that Golightly Man you told me about. Don't you move one single muscle, Bunny Fletcher. I'm on my way over to your house to thresh this out with y'all."

"*No!* Wait—" Listening to the dial tone, Bunny groaned. "Why can't anything ever be simple?"

An hour later Faline was at the door, a slight woman of forty-five in jeans and an oversized gray sweatshirt decorated with lace and flowers. Deep dimples would have been digging holes in her cheeks if she'd been smiling.

"I'm expected at a reception later, so let's straighten this foolishness out real fast," she said as Bunny led her into the living room and seated her on the love seat. "Y'all come sit down and tell me why we can't go into a long and prosperous association. And don't try to palm any BS off onto me, hear?"

"I'm not the same person you offered the position to." Sighing, Bunny sat down and crossed her knees, smoothing down her pink skirt. Faline had been patient and deserved an explanation, so she explained in depth what had happened at the Woodbox. "So, you see, now I feel as if I'm wandering between two worlds, not knowing where I belong."

"Thirty is when everyone begins wonderin' is this *all* there is to life." Faline reached out and squeezed her hand. "I think y'all are fortunate to have grown up more in three months than most women do in a lifetime."

"But I grew down, not up." Bunny gave a humorless laugh. "Remember the rock group Devo? I went through devolution. I thought you were such a feminist you'd think I was insane to want to be a simple housewife and mother."

"Honey, women's rights means every woman should decide what's right for her and be respected for it. If a woman wants to be a wife and mother, no one ought to be makin' her feel guilty." She raised her brows. "Is that what you want?"

"Oh, Lord, now you're asking the questions I don't have answers to." Bunny clapped a hand on her cheek. "It isn't that I have a raving general urge to be a wife and mother. Only with Alec. See, that's how I got into this awful situation. I do want what you're offering too. But neither one or the other seems enough by itself."

"Mmm-*hmmm*." Faline settled back in the love seat, her eyes distant. "Let me put it all into proper perspective. A brilliant woman goes up to work with a troop of retarded people and a Golightly Man. They teach her to relax and enjoy wax dryin' on the floor and bugs bobbin' on a pool. Now she can enjoy the simple pleasures she's never known before, relieving the stress of a competitive career." She nodded. "Can't y'all see it on the big screen?"

"No!" Bunny jumped up as if she'd been stung and began pacing the room, arms crossed over her midriff. "Maybe if there'd been a happy ending . . . but no! Not this way."

Faline glanced at her in exasperation. "Well, y'all are a bright, creative woman. If you want that happy ending badly enough, you'll think of a way."

They both turned when George appeared in the living-room entry arch, home from work for the evening in a charcoal-gray suit and color-coordinated tie and shirt, with every silver-templed hair in place.

"Why, Bunny, you sly thing!" Faline murmured, a smile digging deep dimples into her cheeks. "Who *is* this handsome, sexy man?"

Bunny bestirred herself to make the introductions. "This is my father, George Fletcher. George, Faline Morris."

Faline got up and stepped forward, all southern comfort despite her jeans and sweatshirt. "I've heard everyone singin' the praises of Mr. Promotion hisself all these years! Now I'm finally meetin' you face-to-face."

For once George seemed at a loss for words and wiped his palm on his trousers before taking her hand. "Bunny told me . . . but I didn't expect such a . . ."

"Such a southern belle? I was born and raised in South Carolina, but I hope that won't lead y'all to believe I'm silly."

"Your reputation precedes you," he murmured, his formidable blue eyes turning warm and heavy-lidded.

"And it happens I'm very partial to brilliant, successful women."

Choking on a breath, Bunny felt as if someone had punched her in the stomach. It made her furious to hear her own father using Alec's private flirtatious line. "Faline's schedule is tight, George," she snapped. "She has a reception to attend."

"Honey, in my situation I can change my ol' schedule to fit my whims," Faline said, batting her lashes at George. "If you don't mind your women being forward and liberated, could I talk you into takin' me out to dinner?"

"I would be delighted."

Bunny watched them go out the door, her heart sagging to her toes. If Mr. Prissy could hit it off with a southern belle who was anything but, then obviously everyone in the world was destined to go two by two except her.

A sense of deprivation spurred her into thinking clearly for the first time in weeks. For better or for worse she was going choose the Woodbox world and drop her anchor. She picked up the phone to call Alec but realized he'd forbid her to come.

Then a truly brilliant solution to all their problems went off in her head like a light bulb.

Some two weeks after Frances's visit, insight went off in Alec's mind like a light bulb. For a day he rushed around in a fever making plans, then he called Henry into his office. "The down payment has been sent to Eleganté and the papers should be arriving anytime. I have the factory geared up to turn out the Priceroad commitment. Now I'm resigning as general director."

Henry jumped up. "Why in hell are you backing out?"

"I'm not, I'm moving forward. With the Woodbox success on my résumé, I figure I can make it in southern California." Anxiety twitched Alec's mustache. "However, everything depends upon whether Bunny will take me back. Would you run the factory for a couple weeks while I sail my boat down and kidnap her if necessary, to convince her I'm serious?"

"Sure, but wouldn't it be simpler to make a phone call and set things up?"

Alec stared at him in panic. "You don't understand. I fired her. If I call, she'll probably say I had my chance and that I shouldn't come."

Henry rolled his eyes toward the ceiling. "And I thought retirement was complicated."

FOURTEEN

Launching his boat was something Alec had looked forward to for four years. Now all he felt was impatience as it ran down the ramp and splashed gracefully into the calm waters of the marina. He stepped on board and stood in the cockpit, looking up at the mast and around the teak deck. He was in a manic fever to take her down the coast. His skin prickled with a chill when he wondered if Bunny's feelings for him might have changed now that she was back in her old accelerated environment. Not knowing was torture.

Anxiously he glanced at the clouds building on the horizon. Now that it was September, the weather was chancy again. Hoping to reach the ocean before a storm built up, he fueled the boat and stocked the galley. He'd almost finished when the marina loudspeaker blared, calling him to the phone. Wild with impatience, he ran inside and grabbed the receiver. "Yeah, Golightly here. Whadda you want?"

"This is Henry. Something funny happened. Instead of crediting us with the down payment we sent, Eleganté transferred ownership in total. I called them, and the VP I talked to said an employee paid the remainder in full soon after they received our check for the down payment. The full information is on its way with the papers." Henry paused to contemplate. "I sure as hell can't think of anyone at the Woodbox with that kind of money—must have been a guardian angel from heaven."

"Guardian angel, my left foot!" Alec slammed the flat of his hand against the wall by the phone. "If someone bought controlling interest in a millstone of a factory, you can damn well bet they've got their eye on something more valuable. Like our land, right on the river."

Shifting from foot to foot, he gazed out the window at his boat, aching to forget the Woodbox and its eternal problems for once. Sighing, he knew he couldn't turn his back on the gang. "I'll be there in a few minutes."

Jumping into his Mustang, Alec sped over a bridge and back to the cluster of pale yellow, neatly landscaped factory buildings. Glancing again at the clouds creeping up over the sky, he parked in the Woodbox lot. His heart leaped when he saw a dark, dusty BMW just like Bunny's. But she was back on the fast track, sophisticated again, wearing the peacock-blue jumpsuit and an image like a fort. Making a dash for the main building, he felt a dismal suspicion he'd never fit into her kind of life. Boat or no boat.

He was so preoccupied, he made it to the center of the office before realizing that Bunny actually was standing by the window. Not just a figment of his memories and not a bit sophisticated in skintight jeans and a yellow crop top. Her gold-framed glasses were parked on top of her mane of hair. "Princess . . . ?" he breathed in utter disbelief.

"Yes, it's me," she said softly, going weak with love as she gazed at him. His rugged face was tanned and healthy, but a little gaunt and hollow-eyed, as if he'd missed her too. Gearing for a battle, she set her chin and said, "I didn't like being away from you, so I came back."

"You came back?" Coming to life, Alec leaped forward and crushed her body against his, wrapping himself in her musky scent, the feel of her. "Oh, I missed you so much," he whispered harshly into her hair. "I love you, Bunny, sweetheart."

"I love you, too, darling." Straining against him, she lifted her face to his kiss, the brush of his mustache. Tears flowed down her cheeks, mingling with those on his. After a moment she tilted her head back and gazed into the tropical sea storm of his eyes. "I haven't felt complete since I walked out of this office a month ago."

"You should have, because my soul went with you when you left," he said, kissing her all over her face. "That's why I'm on my way down to Los Angeles to find you."

"But I'm here," she said, frowning questioningly.

A smile trembled on his lips. "I didn't know that until a minute ago. I've resigned from the Woodbox and put my house up for sale. I've had some nibbles, so it shouldn't take long to sell."

"You did what?" she exclaimed, seeing her plans going awry in a few terse statements. "You put the house up for sale! The cottage too?"

"It's a package deal, and only a fantasy, remember?" A smile curved his lips, then died in anxiety. "I decided to take a stab at living up to my potential. Like you'd been been telling me."

Frowning over the burgeoning complications, Bunny touched his flattened nose, his forceful brows, the scar in his chin. "But maybe you're too nice a man to hop on the fast track."

His heart sank. "You're saying you don't think I'll fit into your life down there?"

"No, I'm saying even I don't fit into it, so I . . ." Pulling free, she began pacing the office, trying to think of a way to explain without blowing a deteriorating situation up. "See, I'm attached to the special troop too. I couldn't get Tess and Dwight out of my mind."

"Then you'll be glad to hear he won her parents over by declaring he and Tess were responsible enough to take steps to prevent pregnancy. Now they're planning a simple wedding."

A tender smile lit her face. "I'm so glad."

Alec watched her pace for a moment. "It seems eerie

that you popped up out of nowhere, today of all days, when we're in trouble again."

She stopped short. "What trouble?"

"Someone bought controlling interest in the factory, and God knows what they mean to do with it."

Bunny brushed spiraled wisps of hair off her forehead, then dropped down in the chair behind his desk. "It's not controlling interest, just fifty percent."

He stared blankly at her for several moments. "What are you talking about?"

"I had some money I inherited from my mother and the wages I never spent from the Enterprise, plus the percentage from the Montana movie. So I paid off the Woodbox."

When the full impact penetrated his mind, Alec's initial reaction was anger. "Why didn't you call and tell me you meant to do something this crucial, instead of springing it on me out of the blue?"

Bunny flared right back. "Why didn't you call and tell me you were quitting the Woodbox and selling your house?"

"Because I thought you'd tell me to buzz off."

"That's exactly why I didn't tell you. You were so adamant about my not staying here that I wasn't about to risk you fighting me again."

Alec froze, wondering if she'd bought the Woodbox to punish him for sending her away. "You can't buy into the factory. It's an employee buyout and you aren't one. As I recall, I fired you almost a month ago."

Rising to her feet, Bunny rested her knuckles on the desk. "My contract says I'm an employee through the middle of September, and you didn't have cause to fire me. If you intend to get nasty about it, I now own enough of the factory to fire you if I want to."

"I already quit, remember?" Perching a hip on the front edge of the desk, he studied her intently. Suddenly he realized the dynamic career woman he'd first fallen in love with was revving at full speed underneath the jeans and crop top. "Why the devil did you buy the factory, Bunny?"

"Because I wanted to be with you, no matter what you think is right for me!" She sighed. "But things seem to have boomeranged."

A rush of relief left Alec weak. Everything was going to be all right, but he wanted to hear her say it. "You're still a brilliant, ambitious woman and there's still nothing at the Woodbox to stimulate you."

Bunny sat down in his chair of minor power again. "If you'd discussed the complications instead of springing them on me, we could have worked out solutions. Yes, I'm a bright woman, but if I'd been as ambitious as you think, I wouldn't have come to the Woodbox in the first place. Right?"

"Right." A smile curved his mustache. "You came not once, but three times now."

"I see lots of potential in the Woodbox." She jumped up and began striding around the office, her eyes sparkling with enthusiasm, the words tumbling out of her mouth. "We could put up another building and teach skills to the retarded, with on-the-job training. We can upgrade our product. The Swedish style you laughed about ought to be a natural for kit furniture, using real teak instead of particle board. Or maybe white pine stained to look like teak, since this is Oregon."

"Your plans are workable and very interesting." Smiling, Alec watched his beloved powerhouse pace around his office. There was nothing domestic about her at this point, but he reminded her anyway. "I still can't give you a baby."

Bunny stopped and stared at him, then her face softened in a tender smile. "It takes a lot of time and talent to bring babies up right. We know that from our childhoods. I wouldn't go into it unless I was certain I could be a good mother. Then, if we decided to have a baby, there's always artificial insemination. Right?"

"Right, that occurred to me during one of the nights I lay awake missing you." He gazed at her flawlessly lovely face. "Any other plans and decisions I ought to know about?"

Standing in front of him, Bunny curled a hand around the bare thigh he had cocked over the edge of the desk. She studied his face with meltingly blue eyes. "I thought of a name more fitting for the Woodbox. Styx. S-T-Y-X."

Alec lifted a brow. "Isn't Styx a river in hell?"

"Yes." Her power disappeared in the gentleness of love. "Hell is where I'll be if we can't work this out."

He gathered her into his arms. "I'd go to the ends of the earth to work things out for us. I love you so much, nothing is important except being with you."

"Thank God," she whispered, throwing her arms around his neck in a stranglehold. "I love you so much too."

Kissing her deeply, he absorbed the sweet taste and scent of her. Lifting his head, he touched her face, her hair, settled his hands on the inward curve of her waist. "What happened to the domestic cottage cleaner?"

Bunny laughed softly. "She's still here inside me, Golightly Man. I'm striking a happy medium between two worlds."

He brushed his hands up the slender, erect sweep of her back. "I'm so pleased to hear you say that, sweetheart. By the way, the position of general manager is up for grabs."

"No, I'm a marketing kind of person. Can you think of anyone who might take it, now that you're off to the fast track?" She rested her hands against his muscular chest.

His mustache tipped up at the ends. "It's a dirty job, but I might consider making a comeback. I wasn't looking forward to the rat race anyway, only you."

Bunny studied the askew nose and scarred chin of his past. "There must have been more than me behind your making a decision to leave."

"Yes, insights." Frowning, he walked across the room

to look out the window. "After my mother visited, something pathetic occurred to me. It hurt so bad when my father deserted Carol and me, but I went ahead and sent you away for essentially the same reason. To hide from a genetic flaw."

Bunny stood beside him. "But you did it out of love, not selfishness."

"No matter, I acted like a man I thought I despised all those years." Alec gave a short laugh. "It also came to me that I couldn't have hated him if I was living in his house and driving his old Mustang. I was trying to bring my dad back, I guess. But it didn't work. I don't even like the house, except when you're there."

"Yes, I see why you're selling, darling," Bunny said, nodding. "Happiness isn't a house or a cottage, or a job, or success. It's just us."

"That says it all, Princess." He put his arm around her shoulders. "I take it you gave up Faline?"

"No one gives up Faline," she said, grinning wryly. "Now she's obsessed with putting my story on film. Also, George took one look at her and his dream came true. So, yes, I'd say there'll be a future with Faline."

"You gave up your chance of a lifetime, though."

Bunny kissed the curve of his neck. "My chance of a lifetime is to help you finish your boat and sail into the wild blue yonder."

"Funny you should mention that," Alec said, taking her hand and heading for the door. "Come on."

❖━━━━━━━━❖

Standing on the pier in the marina, Bunny watched Alec's boat move gracefully with the gentle currents in the water. With the sails up for show, it looked like a white swan. He put his arm around her shoulders and nestled his cheek against her hair. "How do you like her name? *Aurora*, after my sleeping beauty."

"I am very touched, darling, but I thought we were going to put fantasies behind us and live in reality."

"Yes, well, let me explain about fantasies." He glanced at the people milling around the marina. "I can explain better on board, in the cabin."

"Oh, great, I'm dying to see it finished." Hopping on deck, she skipped down the companionway ladder. Alec pulled the hatch shut, closing them in a private world of their own, and flipped the lights on with a flourish.

"I don't believe this!" Bunny gasped. Stunned, she walked through the cabin, looking at her floral pictures on the walls, her ruffled pillows on the bunks, her copper kettles in the galley. Her lavender towels and violet-sprigged shower curtain were in the head. Ruffled curtains hung by the port lights. Over the table was a poster of Prince Charming awakening Sleeping Beauty with a kiss.

Coming full circle, she threw her arms around his neck. "It's my ivory tower! Darling, how did I ever survive life before you taught me how to live?"

Hugging her tightly against his body, he whispered, "I shudder to think how close I came to losing you, Princess. My life would have been a wasteland."

"Mine too." She buried her face in his shoulder. "I want to spend all my tomorrows with you."

Alec lifted her face with his fingertips, their eyes meeting. "This is our beginning, no games, no fairy tales. I'm no Prince Charming, just an ordinary guy. And you're a spectac—"

Bunny cut him off. "I'm just an ordinary girl, the glamour thing is a fantasy too."

He nodded. "Will you marry me, Bunny? Let's make *Aurora's* maiden voyage a honeymoon."

"I'd like that more than anything in the world, darling Alec," she said in a husky voice. She swallowed nervously. "There's one thing I have to tell you. I'm . . . thirty-one. Does it bother you that I'm four years older than you are?"

Alec grinned. "I accessed your records and knew from the beginning. But I've lived harder, which makes me much older and wiser."

"And you've been teasing me about it!" she cried out.

His mustache twitched with a restrained laugh. "What are you going to do about it?"

"I'll show you." Grabbing the bottom of his soccer shirt, she stripped it up off his head in one deft motion. Gazing at the pelt of hair covering the muscles of his chest, she lifted a brow. "Have you ever imagined being

Robinson Crusoe, shipwrecked on an isolated island, and I'd be—"

"Wrong fantasy. Friday was a man." Flushed with passion and grinning impishly, Alec took off her clothes piece by piece, then his own until they were standing nude. "Picture this. Tahiti. Adam and Eve in a tropical garden."

"Should I stay away from snakes?" Bunny murmured, glancing down at his body.

"You have a lot to learn about fantasies, Princess." Tangling his fingers in her masses of hair, Alec turned her face up to his kiss. "All the snakes are friendly. And the ever-afters are so happy."

THE EDITOR'S CORNER

There's never too much of a good thing when it comes to romances inspired by beloved stories, so next month we present TREASURED TALES II. Coming your way are six brand-new LOVESWEPTs written by some of the most talented authors of romantic fiction today. You'll delight in their contemporary versions of age-old classics . . . and experience the excitement and passion of falling in love. TREASURED TALES II— what a way to begin the new year!

The first book in our fabulous line up is **PERFECT DOUBLE** by Cindy Gerard, LOVESWEPT #660. In this wonderful retelling of *The Prince and the Pauper* business mogul Logan Prince gets saved by a stranger from a near-fatal mugging, then wakes up in an unfamiliar bed to find a reluctant angel with a siren's body bandaging his wounds! Logan vows to win Carmen Sanchez's heart—

even if it means making a daring bargain with his look-alike rescuer and trading places with the cowboy drifter. It take plenty of wooing before Carmen surrenders to desire—and even more sweet persuasion to regain her trust once he confesses to his charade. A top-notch story from talented Cindy.

Homer's epic poem *The Odyssey* has never been as romantic as Billie Green's version, **BABY, COME BACK**, LOVESWEPT #661. Like Odysseus, David Moore has spent a long time away from home. Finally free after six years in captivity, and with an unrecognizable face and voice, he's not sure if there's still room for him in the lives of his sweet wife, Kathy, and their son, Ben. When he returns home, he masquerades as a handyman, determined to be close to his son, aching to show his wife that, though she's now a successful businesswoman, she still needs him. Poignant and passionate, this love story shows Billie at her finest!

Tom Falconson lives the nightmare of *The Invisible Man* in Terry Lawrence's **THE SHADOW LOVER**, LOVESWEPT #662. When a government experiment goes awry and renders the dashingly virile intelligence agent invisible, Tom knows he has only one person to turn to. Delighted by mysteries, ever in search of the unexplained, Alice Willow opens her door to him, offering him refuge and the sensual freedom to pull her dangerously close. But even as Tom sets out to show her that the phantom in her arms is a flesh-and-blood man, he wonders if their love is strong enough to prove that nothing is impossible. Terry provides plenty of thrills and tempestuous emotions in this fabulous tale.

In Jan Hudson's **FLY WITH ME**, LOVESWEPT #663, Sawyer Hayes is a modern-day Peter Pan who soars through the air in a gleaming helicopter. He touches down in Pip LeBaron's backyard with an offer of a job in his company, but the computer genius quickly informs him that for now she's doing nothing except making up for the childhood she missed. Bewitched by her delicate beauty, Sawyer decides to help her, though her kissable mouth persuades him that a few grown-up games would be more fun. Pip soon welcomes his tantalizing embrace, turning to liquid moonlight beneath his touch. But is there a future together for a man who seems to live for fun and a lady whose work has been her whole life? Jan weaves her magic in this enchanting romance.

"The Ugly Duckling" was Linda Cajio's inspiration for her new LOVESWEPT, **HE'S SO SHY**, #664—and if there ever was an ugly duckling, Richard Creighton was it. Once a skinny nerd with glasses, he's now impossibly sexy, irresistibly gorgeous, and the hottest actor on the big screen. Penelope Marsh can't believe that this leading man in her cousin's movie is the same person she went to grade school with. She thinks he's definitely out of her league, but Richard doesn't agree. Drawn to the willowy schoolteacher, Richard dares her to accept what's written in the stars—that she's destined to be his leading lady for life. Linda delivers a surefire hit.

Last, but certainly not least, is **ANIMAL MAGNETISM** by Bonnie Pega, LOVESWEPT #665. Only Dr. Dolittle is Sebastian Kent's equal when it comes to relating to animals—but Danni Sullivan insists the veterinarian still needs her help. After all, he's new in her hometown, and no one knows every cat, bull, and pig there as well as she. For once giving in to impulse, Sebastian hires her on the spot—then thinks twice about it when her touch arouses long-denied yearnings. He can charm any beast, but he definitely needs a lesson in how to soothe his wounded heart. And Danni has just the right touch to heal his pain—and make him believe in love once more. Bonnie will delight you with this thoroughly enchanting story.

Happy reading!

With warmest wishes,

Nita Taublib

Nita Taublib

Associate Publisher

P.S. Don't miss the fabulous women's fiction Bantam has coming in January: **DESIRE**, the newest novel from bestselling author Amanda Quick; **LONG TIME COMING**, Sandra Brown's classic contemporary romance; **STRANGER IN MY ARMS** by R. J. Kaiser, a novel of romantic suspense in which a woman who has lost her memory is in danger of also losing her life; and **WHERE DOLPHINS GO** by LOVESWEPT author Peggy Webb, a truly unique romance that integrates into its story the fascinating ability of dolphins to aid injured children. We'll be giving you a sneak peek at these wonderful books in next month's LOVESWEPTs. And immediately following this page, look for a preview of the exciting women's novels from Bantam that are *available now!*

Adam's Fall

Available this month in hardcover
from *New York Times*
bestselling author

SANDRA BROWN

Over the past few years, Lilah Mason had watched
her sister Elizabeth find love, get married, and have
children, while she's been more than content to
channel her energies into a career. A physical thera-
pist with an unsinkable spirit and unwavering compassion, she's one of the best in the field. But
when Lilah takes on a demanding new case, her
patient's life isn't the only one transformed. She's
never had a tougher patient than Adam, who challenges her methods and authority at every turn. Yet
Lilah is determined to help him recover the life he's
lost. What she can't see is that while she's winning
Adam's battle, she's losing her heart. Now, as professional duty and passionate yearnings clash, Lilah
must choose the right course for them both.

*Sizzling Romance from One of the
World's Hottest Pens*

Patricia Potter

Nationally bestselling author of
Renegade and **Lightning**

NOTORIOUS

*The owner of the most popular saloon in San Francisco,
Catalina Hilliard knows Marsh Canton is trouble the
moment she first sees him. He's not the first to attempt to
open a rival saloon next door to the Silver Slipper, but he
does possess a steely strength that was missing from the
men she'd driven out of business. Even more perilous to
Cat's plans is the spark of desire that flares between
them, a desire that's about to spin her carefully orchestrated life out of control . . .*

"We have nothing to discuss," she said coldly,
even as she struggled to keep from trembling. All
her thoughts were in disarray. He was so adept at
personal invasion. That look in his eyes of pure radi-
ance, of physical need, almost burned through her.

Fifteen years. Nearly fifteen years since a man
had touched her so intimately. And he was doing
it only with his eyes!

And, dear Lucifer, she was responding.

She'd thought herself immune from desire. If
she'd ever had any, she believed it had been killed

long ago by brutality and shame and utter abhorrence of an act that gave men power and left her little more than a thing to be used and hurt. She'd never felt this bubbling, boiling warmth inside, this craving that was more than physical hunger.

That's what frightened her most of all.

But she wouldn't show it. She would never show it! She didn't even like Canton, devil take him. She didn't like anything about him. And she would send him back to wherever he came. Tail between his legs. No matter what it took. And she would never feel desire again.

But now she had little choice, unless she wished to stand here all afternoon, his hand burning a brand into her. He wasn't going to let her go, and perhaps it was time to lay her cards on the table. She preferred open warfare to guerrilla fighting. She hadn't felt right about the kidnapping and beating—even if she did frequently regret her moment of mercy on his behalf.

She shrugged and his hand relaxed slightly. They left, and he flagged down a carriage for hire. Using those strangely elegant manners that still puzzled her, he helped her inside with a grace that would put royalty to shame.

He left her then for a moment and spoke to the driver, passing a few bills up to him, then returned and vaulted to the seat next to her. Hard-muscled thigh pushed against her leg; his tanned arm, made visible by the rolled-up sleeve, touched her much smaller one, the wiry male hair brushing against her skin, sparking a thousand tiny charges. His scent, a spicy mixture of bay and soap, teased her senses. Everything about him—the strength and power and raw masculinity that he made no attempt to conceal—made her feel fragile, delicate.

But not vulnerable, she told herself. Never vulnerable again. She would fight back by seizing control and keeping it.

She straightened her back and smiled. A seductive smile. A smile that had entranced men for the last ten years. A practiced smile that knew exactly how far to go. A kind of promise that left doors opened, while permitting retreat. It was a smile that kept men coming to the Silver Slipper even as they understood they had no real chance of realizing the dream.

Canton raised an eyebrow. "You *are* very good," he said admiringly.

She shrugged. "It usually works."

"I imagine it does," he said. "Although I doubt if most of the men you use it on have seen the thornier part of you."

"Most don't irritate me as you do."

"Irritate, Miss Cat?"

"Don't call me Cat. My name is Catalina."

"Is it?"

"Is yours really Taylor Canton?"

The last two questions were spoken softly, dangerously, both trying to probe weaknesses, and both recognizing the tactic of the other.

"I would swear to it on a Bible," Marsh said, his mouth quirking.

"I'm surprised you have one, or know what one is."

"I had a very good upbringing, Miss Cat." He emphasized the last word.

"And then what happened?" she asked caustically.

The sardonic amusement in his eyes faded. "A great deal. And what is your story?"

Dear God, his voice was mesmerizing, an intimate song that said nothing but wanted everything. Low and deep and provocative. Compelling. And irresistible . . . almost.

"I had a very poor upbringing," she said. "And then a great deal happened."

For the first time since she'd met him, she saw real humor in his eyes. Not just that cynical amusement as if he were some higher being looking down on a world inhabited by silly children. "You're the first woman I've met with fewer scruples than my own," he said, admiration again in his voice.

She opened her eyes wide. "You have some?"

"As I told you that first night, I don't usually mistreat women."

"Usually?"

"Unless provoked."

"A threat, Mr. Canton?"

"I never threaten, Miss Cat. Neither do I turn down challenges."

"And you usually win?"

"Not usually, Miss Cat. Always." The word was flat. Almost ugly in its surety.

"So do I," she said complacently.

Their voices, Cat knew, had lowered into little more than husky whispers. The air in the closed carriage was sparking, hissing, crackling. Threatening to ignite. His hand moved to her arm, his fingers running up and down it in slow, caressingly sensuous trails.

And then the heat surrounding them was as intense as that in the heart of a volcano. Intense and violent. She wondered very briefly if this was a version of hell. She had just decided it was when he bent toward her, his lips brushing over hers.

And heaven and hell collided.

PRINCESS OF THIEVES
by
Katherine O'Neal

"A brilliant new talent bound to
make her mark on the genre."
—Iris Johansen

*Mace Blackwood is the greatest con artist in the world,
a demon whose family is responsible for the death of
Saranda Sherwin's parents. And though he might be
luring her to damnation itself, Saranda allows herself to be set aflame by the fire in his dark eyes. It's a
calculated surrender that he finds both intoxicating
and infuriating, for one evening alone with the
blue-eyed siren can never be enough. And now he
will stop at nothing to have her forever. . . .*

Saranda could read his intentions in the gleam
of his midnight eyes. "Stay away from me," she
gasped.

"Surely, you're not afraid of me? I've already
admitted defeat."

"As if I'd trust anything you'd say."

Mace raised a brow. "Trust? No, sweetheart, it's
not about trust between us."

"You're right. It's about a battle between our
families that has finally come to an end. The

Sherwins have won, Blackwood. You have no further hand to play."

Even as she said it, she knew it wasn't true. Despite the bad blood between them, they had unfinished business. Because the game, this time, had gone too far.

"That's separate. The feud, the competition—that has nothing to do with what's happening between you and me."

"You must think I'm the rankest kind of amateur. Do you think I don't know what you're up to?"

He put his hand to her cheek and stroked the softly shadowed contours of her face. "What am I up to?"

He was so close, she could feel the muscles of his chest toying with her breasts. Against all sense, she hungered to be touched.

"If you can succeed in seducing me, you can run to Winston with the news—"

His hand drifted from her cheek down the naked column of her neck, to softly caress the slope of her naked shoulder. "I could tell him you slept with me whether you do or not. But you know as well as I do he wouldn't believe me."

"That argument won't work either, Blackwood," she said in a dangerously breathy tone.

"Very well, Miss Sherwin. Why don't we just lay our cards on the table?"

"Why not indeed?"

"Then here it is. I don't like you any more than you like me. In fact, I can't think of a woman I'd be less likely to covet. My family cared for yours no more than yours cared for mine. But I find myself in the unfortunate circumstance of wanting you to distraction. For some reason I can't even fathom, I can't look at you without wondering what you'd look like panting in my arms. Without wanting to feel your naked skin beneath my hands. Or taste your sweat on my tongue. Without needing to come inside you and make you cry out in passion and lose some of that *goddamned* control." A faint moan escaped her throat. "You're all I think about. You're like a fever in my brain. I keep thinking if I took you *just once*, I might finally expel you from my mind. So I don't suppose either of us is leaving this office before we've had what you came for."

"I came to tell you—"

"You could have done that any time. You could have left me wondering for the rest of the night if the wedding would take place. But you didn't wait. You knew if this was going to happen, it had to be tonight. Because once you're Winston's wife, I won't come near you. The minute you say 'I do,' you and I take off the gloves, darling, and the real battle begins. So it's now or never." He lowered his mouth to her shoulder, and her breath left her in a sigh.

"Now or never," she repeated in a daze.

"One night to forget who we are and what it all means. You're so confident of winning. Surely, you wouldn't deny me the spoils of the game. Or more to the point . . . deny yourself."

She looked up and met his sweltering gaze. After three days of not seeing him, she'd forgotten how devastatingly handsome he was. "I shan't fall in love with you, if that's what you're thinking. This will give you no advantage over me. I'm still going after you with both barrels loaded."

"Stop trying so hard to figure it out. I don't give a hang what you think of me. And I don't need your tender mercy. I tell you point-blank, if you think you've won, you may be in for a surprise. But that's beside the point." He wrapped a curl around his finger. Then, taking the pins from her hair, one by one, he dropped them to the floor. She felt her taut nerves jump as each pin clicked against the tile.

He ran both hands through the silvery hair, fluffing it with his fingers, dragging them slowly through the length as he watched the play of light on the silky strands. It spilled like moonlight over her shoulders. "Did you have to be so beautiful?" he rasped.

"Do you have to look so much like a Blackwood?"

He looked at her for a moment, his eyes piercing hers, his hands tangled in her hair. "Tell me what you want."

She couldn't look at him. It brought back memories of his brother she'd rather not relive. As it was, she couldn't believe she was doing this. But she had to have him. It was as elemental as food for her body and air to breathe. Her eyes dropped to his mouth—that blatant, sexual mouth that could make her wild with a grin or wet with a word.

She closed her eyes. If she didn't look at him, maybe she could separate this moment from the past. From what his brother had done. Her voice was a mere whisper when she spoke. "I want you to stop wasting time," she told him, "and make love to me."

He let go of her hair and took her naked shoulders in his hands. Bending her backward, he brought his mouth to hers with a kiss so searing, it scalded her heart.

CAPTURE THE NIGHT

by Geralyn Dawson

Award-winning author of

The Texan's Bride

"My highest praise goes to this author and her work, one of the best . . . I have read in years."
—*Rendezvous*

A desperate French beauty, the ruggedly handsome Texan who rescues her, and their precious stolen "Rose" are swept together by destiny as they each try to escape the secrets of their past.

Madeline groaned as the man called Sinclair sauntered toward her. This is all I need, she thought.

He stopped beside her and dipped into a perfect imitation of a gentleman's bow. Eyes shining, he looked up and said in his deplorable French, "Madame, do you by chance speak English? Apparently, we'll be sharing a spot in line. I beg to make your acquaintance."

She didn't answer.

He sighed and straightened. Then a wicked grin creased his face and in English he drawled, "Brazos Sinclair's my name, Texas born and bred. Most of my friends call me Sin, especially my lady friends. Nobody calls me Claire but once. I'll be sailin' with you on the *Uriel*."

Madeline ignored him.

Evidently, that bothered him not at all. "Cute baby," he said, peeking past the blanket. "Best keep him covered good though. This weather'll chill him."

Madeline bristled at the implied criticism. She glared at the man named Sin.

His grin faded. "Sure you don't speak English?"

She held her silence.

"Guess not, huh. That's all right, I'll enjoy conversin' with you anyway." He shot a piercing glare toward Victor Considérant, the colonists' leader and the man who had refused him a place on the *Uriel*. "I need a diversion, you see. Otherwise I'm liable to do something I shouldn't." Angling his head, he gave her another sweeping gaze. "You're a right fine lookin' woman, ma'am, a real beauty. Don't know that I think much of your husband, though, leavin' you here on the docks by your lonesome."

He paused and looked around, his stare snagging on a pair of scruffy sailors. "It's a dangerous thing for women to be alone in such a place, and for a beautiful one like you, well, I hesitate to think."

Obviously, Madeline said to herself.

The Texan continued, glancing around at the people milling along the wharf. " 'Course, I can't say I understand you Europeans. I've been here goin' on two years, and I'm no closer to figurin' y'all out now than I was the day I rolled off the boat." He reached into his jacket pocket and pulled out a pair of peppermint sticks.

Madeline declined the offer by shaking her head, and he returned one to his pocket before taking a slow lick of the second. "One thing, there's all those kings and royals. I think it's nothin' short of silly to climb on a high horse simply because blood family's been plowin' the same dirt for hundreds of years. I tell you what, ma'am, Texans aren't built for bowin'. It's been bred right out of us."

Brazos leveled a hard stare on Victor Considérant and shook his peppermint in the Frenchman's direction. "And aristocrats are just as bad as royalty. That fellow's one of the worst. Although I'll admit that his head's on right about kings and all, his whole notion to create a socialistic city in the heart of Texas is just plain stupid."

Gesturing toward the others who waited ahead of them in line, he said, "Look around you, lady. I'd lay odds not more than a dozen of these folks know the first little bit about farmin', much less what it takes for survivin' on the frontier. Take that crate, for instance." He shook his head incredulously, "They've stored work tools with violins for an ocean crossing, for goodness sake. These folks don't have the sense to pour rain water from a boot!" He popped the candy into his mouth, folded his arms across his chest, and studied the ship, chewing in a pensive silence.

The nerve of the man, Madeline thought, gritting her teeth against the words she'd love to speak. Really, to comment on another's intelligence when his own is so obviously lacking. Listen to his French.

And his powers of observation. Why, she knew how she looked.

Beautiful wasn't the appropriate word.

Brazos swallowed his candy and said, "Hmm. You've given me an idea." Before Madeline gathered her wits to stop him, he leaned over and kissed her cheek. "Thanks, Beauty. And listen, you take care out here without a man to protect you. If I see your husband on this boat I'm goin' to give him a piece of my mind about leavin' you alone." He winked and left her, walking toward the gangway.

Madeline touched the sticky spot on her cheek damp from his peppermint kiss and watched, fascinated despite herself, as the over-bold Texan tapped Considérant on the shoulder. In French that grated on her ears, he said. "Listen Frenchman, I'll make a deal with you. If you find a place for me on your ship I'll be happy to share my extensive knowledge of Texas with any of your folks who'd be interested in learnin'. This land you bought on the Trinity River—it's not more than half a day's ride from my cousin's spread. I've spent a good deal of time in that area over the past few years. I can tell you all about it."

"Mr. Sinclair," Considérant said in English, "please do not further abuse my language. I chose that land myself. Personally. I can answer any questions my peers may have about our new home. Now, as I have told you, this packet has been chartered to sail La Réunion colonists exclusively. Every space is assigned. I sympathize with your need to return to your home, but unfortunately the *Uriel* cannot accommodate you. Please excuse me, Monsieur Sinclair. I have much to see to before we sail. Good day."

"Good day my—" Brazos bit off his words. He turned abruptly and stomped away from the ship. Halting before Madeline, he declared, "This boat ain't leavin' until morning. It's not over yet. By General Taylor's tailor, when it sails, I'm gonna be on it."

He flashed a victorious grin and drawled, "Honey, you've captured my heart and about three other parts. I'll look forward to seein' you aboard ship."

As he walked away, she dropped a handsome gold pocket watch into her reticule, then called out to him in crisp, King's English. "Better you had offered your brain for ballast, Mr. Sinclair. Perhaps then you'd have been allowed aboard the *Uriel*."

And don't miss these spectacular
romances from Bantam Books,
on sale in December

DESIRE
by the nationally bestselling author
Amanda Quick

LONG TIME COMING
a classic romance by the
New York Times
bestselling author
Sandra Brown

STRANGER IN MY ARMS
a thrilling novel of romantic suspense
by **R. J. Kaiser**

WHERE DOLPHINS GO
by bestselling LOVESWEPT author
Peggy Webb
"Ms. Webb has an inventive mind brimming
with originality that makes all of her
books special reading."
—*Romantic Times*

And in hardcover from Doubleday

AMAZON LILY
by *Theresa Weir*
"Romantic adventure has no finer writer than
the spectacular Theresa Weir."
—*Romantic Times*

OFFICIAL RULES

To enter the sweepstakes below carefully follow all instructions found elsewhere in this offer.

The **Winners Classic** will award prizes with the following approximate maximum values: 1 Grand Prize: $26,500 (or $25,000 cash alternate); 1 First Prize: $3,000; 5 Second Prizes: $400 each; 35 Third Prizes: $100 each; 1,000 Fourth Prizes: $7.50 each. Total maximum retail value of Winners Classic Sweepstakes is $42,500. Some presentations of this sweepstakes may contain individual entry numbers corresponding to one or more of the aforementioned prize levels. To determine the Winners, individual entry numbers will first be compared with the winning numbers preselected by computer. For winning numbers not returned, prizes will be awarded in random drawings from among all eligible entries received. Prize choices may be offered at various levels. If a winner chooses an automobile prize, all license and registration fees, taxes, destination charges and, other expenses not offered herein are the responsibility of the winner. If a winner chooses a trip, travel must be complete within one year from the time the prize is awarded. Minors must be accompanied by an adult. Travel companion(s) must also sign release of liability. Trips are subject to space and departure availability. Certain black-out dates may apply.

The following applies to the sweepstakes named above:

No purchase necessary. You can also enter the sweepstakes by sending your name and address to: P.O. Box 508, Gibbstown, N.J. 08027. Mail each entry separately. Sweepstakes begins 6/1/93. Entries must be received by 12/30/94. Not responsible for lost, late, damaged, misdirected, illegible or postage due mail. Mechanically reproduced entries are not eligible. All entries become property of the sponsor and will not be returned.

Prize Selection/Validations: Selection of winners will be conducted no later than 5:00 PM on January 28, 1995, by an independent judging organization whose decisions are final. Random drawings will be held at 1211 Avenue of the Americas, New York, N.Y. 10036. Entrants need not be present to win. Odds of winning are determined by total number of entries received. Circulation of this sweepstakes is estimated not to exceed 200 million. All prizes are guaranteed to be awarded and delivered to winners. Winners will be notified by mail and may be required to complete an affidavit of eligibility and release of liability which must be returned within 14 days of date on notification or alternate winners will be selected in a random drawing. Any prize notification letter or any prize returned to a participating sponsor, Bantam Doubleday Dell Publishing Group, Inc., its participating divisions or subsidiaries, or the independent judging organization as undeliverable will be awarded to an alternate winner. Prizes are not transferable. No substitution for prizes except as offered or as may be necessary due to unavailability, in which case a prize of equal or greater value will be awarded. Prizes will be awarded approximately 90 days after the drawing. All taxes are the sole responsibility of the winners. Entry constitutes permission (except where prohibited by law) to use winners' names, hometowns, and likenesses for publicity purposes without further or other compensation. Prizes won by minors will be awarded in the name of parent or legal guardian.

Participation: Sweepstakes open to residents of the United States and Canada, except for the province of Quebec. Sweepstakes sponsored by Bantam Doubleday Dell Publishing Group, Inc., (BDD), 1540 Broadway, New York, NY 10036. Versions of this sweepstakes with different graphics and prize choices will be offered in conjunction with various solicitations or promotions by different subsidiaries and divisions of BDD. Where applicable, winners will have their choice of any prize offered at level won. Employees of BDD, its divisions, subsidiaries, advertising agencies, independent judging organization, and their immediate family members are not eligible.

Canadian residents, in order to win, must first correctly answer a time limited arithmetical skill testing question. Void in Puerto Rico, Quebec and wherever prohibited or restricted by law. Subject to all federal, state, local and provincial laws and regulations. For a list of major prize winners (available after 1/29/95): send a self-addressed, stamped envelope entirely separate from your entry to: Sweepstakes Winners, P.O. Box 517, Gibbstown, NJ 08027. Requests must be received by 12/30/94. DO NOT SEND ANY OTHER CORRESPONDENCE TO THIS P.O. BOX.

Don't miss these fabulous Bantam women's fiction titles

now on sale

• NOTORIOUS

by Patricia Potter, author of *RENEGADE*

Long ago, Catalina Hilliard had vowed never to give away her heart, but she hadn't counted on the spark of desire that flared between her and her business rival, Marsh Canton. Now that desire is about to spin Cat's carefully orchestrated life out of control.
_____56225-8 $5.50/6.50 in Canada

• PRINCESS OF THIEVES

by Katherine O'Neal, author of *THE LAST HIGHWAYMAN*

Mace Blackwood was a daring rogue—the greatest con artist in the world. Saranda Sherwin was a master thief who used her wits and wiles to make tough men weak. And when Saranda's latest charade leads to tragedy and sends her fleeing for her life, Mace is compelled to follow, no matter what the cost.
_____56066-2 $5.50/$6.50 in Canada

• CAPTURE THE NIGHT

by Geralyn Dawson

In this "Once Upon a Time" Romance with "Beauty and the Beast" at its heart, Geralyn Dawson weaves the love story of a runaway beauty, the Texan who rescues her, and their precious stolen "Rose."
_____56176-6 $4.99/5.99 in Canada

Ask for these books at your local bookstore or use this page to order.

❑ Please send me the books I have checked above. I am enclosing $ _____ (add $2.50 to cover postage and handling). Send check or money order, no cash or C. O. D.'s please.

Name _____

Address _____

City/ State/ Zip _____

Send order to: Bantam Books, Dept. FN123, 2451 S. Wolf Rd., Des Plaines, IL 60018
Allow four to six weeks for delivery.
Prices and availability subject to change without notice.